PUFFIN BOOKS

SPY DOG
Rollercoaster!

My dog can find anything. She's a Labra*Google*! Geddit? No? Oh.

Well, the truth is that my dog is rubbish. She never Googles anything. She's called Lara. She sleeps a lot and makes bad doggy smells. She certainly doesn't go on my PS3 or Wii. And she absolutely cannot ride a motorbike or eat spag Bol with a knife and fork. And as for riding on rollercoasters! That'd be ridiculous. Wouldn't it?

If you want Spy Dog to come to your school, please email her at lara@artofbrilliance.co.uk. She'll probably have to bring Andrew Cope along because she feels a bit sorry for him. He doesn't get out much, you see. I know you'll make a fuss of Lara. Please, please make a big fuss of Andrew too.

www.spydog451.co.uk

SPY DOG

Rollercoaster!

ANDREW COPE

Illustrated by James de la Rue

PUFFIN

PUFFIN BOOKS

Published by the Penguin Group
Penguin Books Ltd, 80 Strand, London WC2R ORL, England
Penguin Group (USA) Inc., 375 Hudson Street, New York, New York 10014, USA
Penguin Group (Canada), 90 Eglinton Avenue East, Suite 700, Toronto, Ontario, Canada M4P 2Y3
(a division of Pearson Penguin Canada Inc.)
Penguin Ireland, 25 St Stephen's Green, Dublin 2, Ireland (a division of Penguin Books Ltd)
Penguin Group (Australia), 707 Collins Street, Melbourne, Victoria 3008, Australia
(a division of Pearson Australia Group Pty Ltd)
Penguin Books India Pvt Ltd, 11 Community Centre, Panchsheel Park, New Delhi – 110 017, India
Penguin Group (NZ), 67 Apollo Drive, Rosedale, Auckland 0632, New Zealand
(a division of Pearson New Zealand Ltd)
Penguin Books (South Africa) (Pty) Ltd, Block D, Rosebank Office Park, 181 Jan Smuts Avenue,
Parktown North, Gauteng 2193, South Africa

Penguin Books Ltd, Registered Offices: 80 Strand, London WC2R ORL, England

puffinbooks.com

First published 2012
This edition published 2012
001

Set in Bembo
Typeset by Palimpsest Book Production Limited, Falkirk, Stirlingshire
Printed in Great Britain by Clays Ltd, St Ives plc

British Library Cataloguing in Publication Data
A CIP catalogue record for this book is available from the British Library

ISBN: 978-0-141-34560-4

www.greenpenguin.co.uk

Penguin Books is committed to a sustainable
future for our business, our readers and our planet.
This book is made from Forest Stewardship
Council™ certified paper.

MIX
Paper from
responsible sources
FSC™ C018179
www.fsc.org

ALWAYS LEARNING   **PEARSON**

Contents

1. Pick-pocket

Enchanted Towers Theme Park was doing magical business. At ten o'clock in the morning it was already packed; the air rang with happy screams, there were queues for all the big rides and more visitors were streaming in through the main gates.

'What do you want to go on first?' a mother asked her three children as they pushed through the turnstiles.

'The Fee-Fi-Fo-Fum ride,' said one boy. 'It's amazing! You whizz round the beanstalk so fast your eyes nearly pop out of your head!'

'Nah! Let's do the Rollertoaster,' said his brother. 'You go down and down and it gets hotter and hotter until you suddenly pop up!'

'What about Rapunzel's Tower? That's got to be the best. See how high it is?' The first boy pointed to a tall, thin tower rising above the treetops. 'And they dangle you over the edge for ages before they drop you!'

'Yeah, OK.' His brother nodded in agreement. 'Rapunzel's Tower.'

'What about you, sweetie?' asked the mother, bending down to the little girl. 'What do you want to do first?'

'I want to meet Princess Pretty and her Troll Prince. They're my favourites.'

Both boys stuck fingers in their mouths and made gagging noises.

'Oh, look!' cried the little girl, ignoring her brothers. 'There they are!'

A beautiful, dark-haired girl stood in the square beyond the turnstiles, dressed in a pink princess costume. An enormous troll with a snaggle-toothed smile stood beside her. He was dressed like a prince and had a tiny crown perched on the top of his huge head.

The little girl let go of her mother's hand and raced towards her fairy-tale heroes.

'Oof!' said Princess Pretty as the little girl cannoned into her.

'Sorry,' said the mother, catching up. 'She's been dying to meet you. She loves Princess

Pretty and her Troll Prince, don't you, sweetie?'

'Well, we love you too. We surely do!' said Princess Pretty brightly, yanking her dress out of the little girl's sticky grip.

'She's got the storybook, the dolls, everything,' the mother said. 'She loves the bit where your troll turns into a handsome prince.'

'How sweet,' said Princess Pretty, eyeing the mother's open handbag. A purse was sticking out of the top.

The mother turned away to check on her boys, and Princess Pretty took her chance. Patting the little girl on the head with one hand, she lifted the purse from the mother's bag with the other and passed it to the Troll Prince. Quickly, he pushed it into his snaggle-toothed mouth just before the mother turned back.

'Bye-bye now!' called Princess Pretty as the little family headed for the rides. 'Have a nice day!'

'They won't though, will they?' groaned a voice from inside the troll's massive chest. 'Because we've stolen all their spending money.'

Princess Pretty glared at the troll. 'Don't start that again, Darren,' she hissed under her breath.

'But I feel really bad!' wailed Darren from inside the troll suit. 'Let's give the purse back. We can say she dropped it –'

Princess Pretty stamped her foot. 'Don't you care about me?'

'Of course I do, Princess! More than anything in the world, but . . .'

Princess Pretty narrowed her beautiful eyes. 'But?'

'But I don't want to help you pick any more pockets,' Darren blurted. 'Please don't make me.'

'So, how are we going to get enough cash for me to go to Hollywood and become a star? Hmm?' demanded Princess Pretty.

Darren shrugged inside his troll suit. 'Maybe we should just stay here. It's not so bad.'

'Not so bad? You can't be serious! I hate this place, I hate this job and I especially hate wearing this silly pink princess outfit!'

'You should try wearing a troll suit,' muttered Darren. 'It's like an oven in here and this head weighs a ton.'

'Be quiet!' snarled Princess Pretty. 'This isn't about you!'

'It never is,' sighed Darren. 'It's always about you.'

Princess Pretty was about to tear a strip off Darren when she spotted a white-haired man in a brightly coloured waistcoat heading towards them. 'Watch out. The boss is coming,' she hissed, turning her snarl into a smile. 'Good morning, Mr Cartwright!'

'I've been watching you two,' said Mr Cartwright.

Darren groaned inside his troll suit. 'We're so sorry, boss. We'll give it back straight aw—OWWW!'

Mr Cartwright raised a bushy eyebrow. 'Are you all right, son?'

'He's fine,' said Princess Pretty, grinding the heel of her shoe deeper into Darren's foot. 'Aren't you?'

'Ye-es!' squeaked Darren.

'Good. As I was saying, I've been watching you two, and it's clear that Princess Pretty and her Troll Prince are very popular with our visitors. I think you deserve a reward for all your hard work.'

'Why thank you, Mr Cartwright,' sang Princess Pretty, her eyelids fluttering. 'We just love seeing the happy faces of the little kiddies . . . Hang on. Did you say "reward"?' Princess Pretty's eyes gleamed greedily. 'What reward?'

'In two days' time we launch our latest ride.' Mr Cartwright nodded proudly towards the Enchanted Towers woods, where the gleaming curves of the new rollercoaster rose above the treetops. 'It's going to be the longest, twirliest, fastest rollercoaster in the world!'

'Wonderful,' said Princess Pretty, willing him to get to the reward part.

'As you know, we held a competition to find a name for our new rollercoaster,' continued Mr Cartwright. 'And I have just chosen the winner. I'll be telling him this afternoon and he will arrive at Enchanted Towers this evening, along with his family.'

'And my reward is . . .?' Princess Pretty prompted.

'Ah yes. I have chosen you two to be the face of Enchanted Towers for this very special event!' said Mr Cartwright.

'That's it?' said Princess Pretty. 'THAT'S IT?! I mean . . . how very – lovely.' She made a deep curtsy to hide her angry face.

Mr Cartwright carried on happily. 'I know! It's a real honour. Not only will you be looking after our competition winner and his family, but you'll also be taking care of another very special guest. Chart-topping singer Summer Rayne will be coming here to launch our new ride!'

Princess Pretty rose up out of her curtsy, her eyes glittering with a mad mixture of hatred and joy. 'Summer Rayne?' she hissed.

Mr Cartwright beamed. 'Pop sensation Summer Rayne! She's a *real* superstar. We're very lucky to get her.'

'Wow! What are the chances, Princess?' said Darren.

Princess Pretty ignored him.

'Chances?' asked Mr Cartwright. 'What do you mean, Darren?'

'Princess knows Summer Rayne!' explained Darren. 'Owww! My foot!'

Princess Pretty gave a tinkly laugh. 'Don't be silly, Darren. I don't know her. I just *feel* as though I know her because she's so famous.'

'But I thought you were in the same – OWWW!'

'For instance, I know the words to all her hit songs,' continued Princess Pretty, giving Darren's foot another jab.

'Excellent! It sounds as though you're just

the person to take care of her,' said Mr Cartwright.

'Oh, I'll take care of *her* all right,' growled Princess Pretty.

Beep! Beep! Beep!

Mr Cartwright unhooked his pager from his belt and frowned at the screen. 'Oh no,' he breathed, turning pale. 'Another visitor's purse has gone missing.'

'That's our fault,' moaned Darren as Mr Cartwright headed off. 'I feel terrible.'

'Don't worry, wimp,' snapped Princess Pretty. 'We don't need to pick any more pockets. I have a cunning plan. Summer Rayne is going to give me all the money I need, and more.'

2. Spies!

'I'm afraid it's now or never,' woofed Lara. 'Are you ready, pups?'

'But, the Prof isn't here yet!' whimpered Star. 'We can't go ahead without him!'

'We have no choice,' said Lara. 'In five minutes' time this place will be overrun; we won't stand a chance of getting across unseen.'

Star's sticky-up ear drooped and Spud's tail crept between his legs. Lara understood exactly how her pups were feeling. Professor Cortex might be one of the world's top scientists and the head of the British Government's animal spying programme, but he had always found time to be there for the important moments in their lives. He had trained Lara to be the world's first ever Spy Dog and, once she had retired from active service, he had trained her pups too.

He had been there, beaming with pride, when Spud and Star became fully fledged Spy Dogs.

So where was her old friend now?

Lara sighed. 'Sorry, pups. We can't wait any longer.'

'Chin up, sis,' woofed Spud, touching his nose to Star's. 'Even if the Prof isn't here to see it, we're still about to do something amazing!'

Star's sticky-up ear sprang to attention again. 'You're right,' she barked. 'The world's first ever dog free-runners. We've been training for this for weeks. Come on, let's do it!'

They were in the playground of their local park. Quickly, Star turned to face the big slide, Spud ran to stand behind her and Lara took her place behind Spud, checking to see if anyone was watching as she went. In a few minutes' time, the park would fill up with children when the school next door finished for the summer but, for now, there were only three people to be seen, and none of them were interested in Lara and her pups. The old lady on the bench was reading a newspaper, the park gardener was weeding a flower bed with his back to them and the homeless man sprawled in the shade of a tree was snoring loudly. Lara gave a satisfied nod.

'Ready, pups?'

'Ready, Ma,' yapped Star, going into a crouch.

Spud waggled his rear end. 'Ready, Ma!'

'Remember, keep moving and don't touch the ground. You get marks for style as well as skill. Spud, wait three seconds before you follow Star. I'll bring up the rear. Go, Star!'

Star raced for the slide like a black and white arrow.

'One, two, three! Geronimo!' yapped Spud, charging after his sister.

Lara counted off three more seconds before following Spud as fast as her paws would go.

Star galloped up the slippery slide chute to the top and then flung herself over the edge. She fell towards a climbing frame, but twisted in mid-air, hit the top platform with all four paws and pushed off again. *Full marks for style!* This time, she tumbled towards a rocking horse and landed on the saddle. The horse tipped on its spring and then –

Boing!

– it bounced back, shooting Star into the air again. She somersaulted and came down neatly on the roof of the playhouse.

'Yeehah!' yapped Spud, bouncing off the rocking horse saddle. 'Good free-running, sis!'

'Thanks, pardner,' Star panted, vaulting on to the playhouse chimney.

The next jump was the most difficult of all, but Star didn't hesitate. She leapt from the chimney to the see-saw, landed on the lower seat and then ran up the sloping bar towards the higher seat. As she passed the mid-point, the see-saw tipped, and she slid the rest of the way down the bar.

'Here I come!' yapped Spud.

Star scrambled on to the seat just as her brother jumped from the playhouse chimney and landed with a thud on the other end of the see-saw. His seat shot down and Star's seat shot up, catapulting her across the final stretch of the playground and on to the grass beyond.

Star rolled as she landed and then came up on to her back legs, like a gymnast at the end of her routine. *Chest out. Bum out. Arms high!* 'That was amazing!'

'My turn!' called Spud, galloping along to the other end of the see-saw. He reached the far seat just as Lara jumped from the playhouse on to the see-saw and sent him flying through the air like a furry black cannonball. Lara's extra weight sent him much higher than his sister. 'Whoo-hoo!' he howled, flying through the air. 'Is it a bird . . . or a plane?'

Star put her paw to her eyes to shield them from the sun. She gulped as her brother soared through the blue sky.

'No, it's a superdooooog,' she heard him yowl before he disappeared over the school fence. There was a splash as the puppy landed in the school's outdoor pool.

Lara looked at Star who blinked back, rather alarmed.

'No harm done,' wagged Spud as his soggy body emerged from under the school fence. 'Practised my front crawl too!' The puppy shook his body, water spraying everywhere. 'You saw it here, folks!' he yapped. 'Dogs really can fly!'

'Uh-oh,' woofed Star, suddenly serious. 'There could be trouble on the way.'

Lara and Spud turned to see the old lady from the bench heading towards them.

Lara frowned. 'Hmm. She either saw us free-running, or she's coming to shoo us off the grass.'

'Should we make a run for it?' asked Spud.

'We can't!' Lara barked. 'We're meeting Ben, Sophie and Ollie here when they finish school – and they'll be arriving any minute,' she added as the school bell finished ringing from across the road.

'What do we do, Ma?' asked Star.

'Stay put,' woofed Lara, watching the old lady totter on to the playground. 'Maybe she just wants to make friends.'

Suddenly the old lady wobbled off her high heels and fell over with a loud squawk. As Lara, Spud and Star ran to help, the old lady's skirt flapped up over her face.

'She's got *really* hairy legs,' yapped Star, skidding to a stop beside the old lady.

'And she's wearing lime-green Y-fronts!' yelped Spud.

'That's because she's no lady,' growled Lara, glaring down at the man in disguise. 'Someone's been spying on us!'

3. School's Out!

Lara scanned the park. Now the homeless man and the gardener were both hurrying towards the playground too. *Who* are *these people?* she thought. She was about to yank the skirt from the imposter's face when a familiar voice spoke from beneath the flowery material.

'Hello, GM451.'

Lara gasped. Only one person used her Spy Dog code name. 'It's Professor Cortex!' she woofed.

'Yay! He did come to see us – I knew he wouldn't let us down!' yapped Star.

'But why's he dressed like a gruesome grannie?' asked Spud.

Professor Cortex sat up and straightened his wig. 'I'll never understand why women choose to wear such painful and, frankly, dangerous footwear,' he grumbled, scowling at his high heels. 'Help me up, please.'

Spud grabbed one sleeve of the professor's frilly blouse and Star grabbed the other.

'Heave, pups!' woofed Lara, putting her shoulder against his back. Professor Cortex staggered to his feet and pulled his skirt down over his hairy legs as the homeless man and the park gardener arrived.

'Ah, Agents K and T,' he said. 'Good undercover work.'

'Thank you, sir,' said the professor's personal bodyguards, pulling their shades from their pockets and slipping them on. 'Looks like we fooled our three Spy Dogs!'

Lara gaped at the hairy homeless man and the park gardener and then slapped a paw to her forehead. *How could I have missed them?*

'Yes, you might well feel ashamed of yourself, GM451,' glared Professor Cortex. 'You may be retired now, but your pups will be going into active service soon. You should be passing on all your training to them – including observational skills!'

Lara hung her head. *It's true; I've lost my edge.* Since she had given up being a Spy Dog and moved in with the Cook family as their family pet, she had become just a bit too comfortable.

Cheering and a stampede of footsteps saved her from one of the professor's lectures.

'Yikes!' yapped Spud. 'School's out for summer!'

He pointed at the gates just as a herd of cheering children burst into the park and thundered towards the playground, throwing their school bags away as they ran.

'No way!' yelped Professor Cortex, watching the crowd stampeding towards him. 'Get me out of here! I can't run in these shoes!'

Agents K and T picked up the professor by his elbows and quick-marched him off the playground. As Lara followed, head down, she heard someone shouting her name.

'Lara!'

She turned, and saw Ben running towards her, followed by Sophie and Ollie. Suddenly she felt a whole lot better. Lara loved all the members of the Cook family, but she and

Ben had a special bond, plus he didn't give two hoots about her losing her Spy Dog skills.

'Summer holidays, Lara!' Ben yelled, giving her a fierce hug. 'Six weeks to do whatever we want! Football, fishing, camping . . . brilliant!'

And barbecues! wagged Lara.

'Brilliant!' yelled Ollie, grabbing Spud and wrestling him to the ground. 'Yuk, you're all wet!' Spud wriggled out of Ollie's grip, jumped on to his chest and planted his paws on his shoulders.

Victory for the soggy doggy! Get out of that!

'Brothers,' said Sophie, sitting down beside Star. 'Who'd have 'em?'

Star leant against her. *Tell me about it!*

'Where's the Prof?' asked Ben. 'I thought he was coming to watch you three do your free-running?'

Lara raised an eyebrow and nodded her head towards Professor Cortex. *Check out the skirt and handbag combo.*

Ben, Sophie and Ollie stared, open-mouthed.

'Ah yes. I can explain,' spluttered Professor Cortex, straightening his wig. 'My agents and I came here in disguise.'

'Why?' asked Ben.

'To test our Spy Dogs' observational skills,' said Professor Cortex. 'They failed, I'm afraid. You'll have to work on that, GM451.'

Don't worry, Prof. I'm on it! Lara scanned the park through narrowed eyes, wishing she had her reading glasses with her.

'However,' the professor continued, 'their free-running was very impressive. And the little fella's swimming is coming on nicely too! So, well done, Lara. You did exactly as instructed.'

Lara dipped her head modestly, but she

22

knew she had done a good job. Spud's love of food had been starting to show on his waist-line, so Professor Cortex had asked her to get her pup into shape. Admittedly, there had been a few false starts. Instead of exercising on Mrs Cook's treadmill in the garage, Spud had recorded himself running on it, and had then left the recording playing while he sneaked off to play computer games with Ollie. Lara had tried cross-country runs next, but Spud had simply given up and caught the bus home.

'It's so boring!' he had whined, each time he was found out.

So Lara had tried something that would exercise Spud's brain as well as his body: free-running. Spud had taken to it instantly. He loved the challenge of racing along, scaling walls and vaulting over obstacles.

'It's like a computer game, Ma!' he had yapped. 'You have to keep looking ahead and working out exactly when to jump and where to put your paws next. I love it!'

They had been in training ever since, and all three of them had become fitter. There was only one problem: Spud's muscles had grown bigger, but so had his appetite.

'Trouble to our left,' said Agent K, breaking into Lara's thoughts. Two people were standing beside the flower bed where Agent T had been digging.

I should've spotted them first, Lara thought. *I really must sharpen up!*

'That's the real park gardener,' said Ben.

'And she's got a policeman with her,' Ollie added.

The gardener was pointing at the flower bed and waving her arms about.

'She doesn't look too happy,' said Agent T. 'Maybe some of those weeds I dug up weren't weeds after all.'

'Come on, everyone,' said Professor Cortex as the gardener and the police officer looked their way. 'Time for a quick exit.'

Or as quick as you can go in those shoes, thought Lara.

They hurried out of the park with Agents T and K supporting Professor Cortex as he tottered along on his high heels. A black Secret Service van was parked on the street outside. Professor Cortex clambered into the back and sat down on one of the luxurious leather seats with a grateful sigh. Lara, Spud,

Star and the children piled in after him, and Agents T and K shut the doors before climbing into the front of the van.

'Activate the external cameras,' ordered Professor Cortex.

Agent K pressed a button and the van's monitor screens lit up, showing the street outside. The police officer and the park gardener were already through the park gates and sprinting towards the van.

'Put your foot down, Agent T!' the professor shouted. 'Now!'

The van pulled away from the kerb with a screech of tyres and shot off down the street, leaving their pursuers far behind.

'Where to, sir?' asked Agent T.

'The Cooks' house,' ordered Professor Cortex, easing out of his high heels and unbuttoning his frilly blouse. 'And go the long way round, to give us time to get out of our disguises.'

Phew! I think we've had our share of excitement for the day, thought Lara as the van sped towards home.

4. Storm Spell!

'Our garden's full of people!' Ollie cried as the van pulled up outside the house. 'And one of them is massive!'

Lara looked at the van's monitor screens. There were seven people packed on to the little square of grass at the front of the Cooks' house. Mr and Mrs Cook were there, as well as a man with a camera and a woman with a notebook. Next to them stood an old man with long, white hair and a colourful waistcoat, a beautiful, dark-haired girl dressed as a princess and a – Lara frowned at the screen. *What is that?*

'A troll!' cried Sophie. 'Look! There's a troll in our garden!'

'Really?' said Ollie in an interested voice. 'I thought they lived under bridges. Do they eat people?'

27

'It's not a real troll,' Sophie explained. 'It's somebody dressed up as a troll.'

'Oh.' Ollie sounded disappointed. 'But why is he in our garden?'

'I think I might know,' said Ben, with a quiver of excitement in his voice. 'Come on, Lara. Let's go and find out.'

'Ah! Here are the children!' cried Mrs Cook as they all climbed from the van and squeezed into the front garden. 'Looks like they got a lift home from –'

'– from their grandfather,' interrupted Professor Cortex, eyeing the pair with the camera and the notebook. 'Yes. I am their grandfather. And these two,' he added as Agents T and K took up their positions on either side of him, 'are their uncles.'

Mrs Cook looked surprised, but recovered quickly. 'That's right,' she said in a slightly high voice. 'Grandfather.'

'And uncles,' said Mr Cook, nodding furiously.

There was an awkward pause. Lara glanced anxiously between the journalists and Ollie. At twelve and ten, Ben and Sophie were old enough to understand why Professor Cortex was hiding his true identity, but Ollie was only six. Would he blow the Prof's cover? Luckily, he was too busy staring up at the troll to bother about anything else.

'Which one of you boys is Ben?' asked the white-haired old man.

'That's me,' said Ben.

'Pleased to meet you, son!' said the old man. 'My name is Mr Cartwright and I own Enchanted Towers Theme Park. Can you guess why I'm here?'

'I think so,' said Ben shyly, glancing across at his mum and dad. Mr Cook was beaming proudly, and Mrs Cook had gone a pretty shade of pink.

'We asked people to send in names for our new mega-rollercoaster ride. I'm pleased to announce that you, Ben, are the winner, with your brilliant suggestion, "Storm Spell".'

Ben grinned as Mr Cartwright shook his hand, and everyone clapped and cheered

'Your prize,' Mr Cartwright continued, 'is a two-night stay in the Enchanted Towers Hotel for you and your family, a two-day pass giving access to all the rides in the park, plus seats in the front carriage for the launch of Storm Spell!'

'Yay!' Ollie yelled at the top of his lungs. The garden was too crowded for him to run around, so he contented himself with jumping up and down on the spot, chanting, 'Storm Spell! Storm Spell! Storm Spell!'

'Enchanted Towers!' cried Sophie. 'What a brilliant start to the summer holidays!'

'Your dogs can come too, of course,' said Mr Cartwright, patting Lara on the head. 'But we won't be giving them passes for the rides; we don't want to terrify the poor things.'

Lara raised an eyebrow. *What a cheek! I've ridden a space rocket – on the outside! A few theme park rides won't frighten me.* But she allowed Mr

Cartwright to keep patting her because she knew he was only being kind.

'During your stay with us you'll be looked after by Princess Pretty and her Troll Prince,' explained Mr Cartwright.

Princess Pretty made a deep curtsy and the Troll Prince gave them a wave.

'Last but not least,' said Mr Cartwright, 'chart-topping singer, Summer Rayne, will be launching the Storm Spell ride for us, and you'll all get to meet her!'

The press photographer's camera flashed again and the reporter scribbled furiously in her notebook.

'When do we go?' asked Ben.

'Your adventure starts tonight, Ben,' said Mr Cartwright. 'The Enchanted Towers Hotel is awaiting your arrival. Tomorrow, you'll spend the day enjoying the theme park and, in the evening, you'll have VIP seats for Summer Rayne's show in our theatre. Then, on Sunday, you will be our special guests for the launch of Storm Spell!'

'We've already packed,' said Mr Cook, pointing to the suitcases strapped to the top of their car. 'All you lot need to do is get changed and grab anything else you want to take.'

'Computer games!' yelled Ollie, pushing through the throng and rushing into the house.

'Ollie!' cried Mrs Cook. 'Where are your manners?'

'No, he's quite right,' laughed Mr Cartwright. 'There's no time to lose! Go and get sorted, everyone. We'll see you later at Enchanted Towers.'

Mr Cartwright waved the Cooks into the house and then turned to leave, but the reporter stepped in front of him.

'Mr Cartwright, would you care to comment on the pick-pocketing plague at Enchanted Towers? I'm sure the *Daily Dose* readers would like to hear your side of the story.'

The troll, who had been completely silent until now, let out a whimper.

'Be quiet, Darren!' hissed Princess Pretty, giving the troll a vicious pinch on the arm.

Hmm, Lara thought, seeing the pinch. *It seems our Princess Pretty has a nasty streak.*

Mr Cartwright looked upset. 'There have been a few incidents,' he admitted, stepping out on to the street and heading for the

Enchanted Towers official car. 'But I have compensated every victim and we are working hard to solve the problem.'

Princess Pretty and the Troll Prince hurried after Mr Cartwright and the *Daily Dose* reporters. Lara, Spud and Star were left alone in the garden with Professor Cortex and his agents.

'Well, well, well. Pick-pockets, eh?' said Professor Cortex. 'Lara, Spud, Star, I think you've just been handed your next mission.'

Lara nodded her agreement. *Sounds as though Enchanted Towers needs a bit of Spy Dog magic!*

'It'll be a chance to work on our observational skills,' yapped Star.

'Wait right there,' said the professor. 'I have the perfect gadget.'

He hurried to the van, rummaged in the back and returned carrying three pink heart lockets. 'These might look like pretty bits of jewellery, but they're solar-powered miniature camcorders,' he explained. 'When you want to watch the footage you've recorded, all you need to do is find a laptop and . . .'

The professor took hold of the point of the heart and pulled. It came away, revealing a plug-in for a laptop.

'Very clever!' yapped Spud, who loved gadgets. 'Pity it's pink.'

'So, if you spot a pick-pocket, there's no need for any heroics,' said Professor Cortex. 'Simply catch them on camera, then hand over the evidence to the Enchanted Park security people. The camcorders automatically switch to infra-red in the dark, so you can film at night too.'

Professor Cortex attached lockets to Lara and Star's collars and then he turned to Spud.

'No way!' yapped Spud, backing away from the pink, glittery heart.

'Ah yes. Sorry about the girly bling, Spud,' said the professor. 'We've been trying to catch a certain master-criminal for ages, but he's very good at covering his tracks. His new girlfriend adores cats, though, so we're planning to send her three cute kittens as a gift, each one of them wearing a camcorder locket. After a few days, I think we'll have all the evidence we need to arrest our guy. Operation Kittie doesn't start until next month, so you could borrow these for the weekend.'

Professor Cortex held out the glittery locket again. Spud scowled and kept his distance. *You might be happy dressing like a girl, Prof, but I'm not!*

'Come on, Spud,' woofed Lara. 'It's for the good of the mission.'

With a resigned growl, Spud allowed the professor to clip the locket to his collar.

'Suits you, Spud!' yapped Star. 'The pink really sets off your black fur.'

'Are you laughing at me?' asked Spud suspiciously.

'I wouldn't do that! After all, us girls have to stick together.'

Luckily for Star, the Cook family hurried out of the house just as Spud was about to give her sticky-up ear a good twist.

'Where'd you get the pretty matching lockets?' asked Mrs Cook as they piled into the car.

Lara looked at Professor Cortex and shook her head. *Don't mention the pick-pockets. I want this to be the best possible weekend for Ben and the rest of the Cook family.*

To her relief, Professor Cortex seemed to have come to the same conclusion. 'Oh, those. They're prototype gadget cases. Lara, Spud and Star are going to wear them for the weekend, just to see how hard-wearing they are,' he called, waving goodbye as he headed back to his van.

Lara settled on to the blankets in the back of the car with a relieved sigh. With any luck, everyone would get something out of their stay at Enchanted Towers. The Cook family would have a lovely holiday, Lara and her pups could get down to some serious detective work and Mr Cartwright would have the pleasure of handing the

Enchanted Towers pick-pocket over to the police.

'Mission Pick-pocket, here we come!' woofed Lara.

5. Star Treatment

Mr Cartwright led the Cook family along the tenth-floor corridor of the Enchanted Towers Hotel to the 'Wizard's Suite'. He swiped a key card through the slot and the door swung open on soundless hinges.

'Welcome to your home for the next two nights.'

'Whoa! It's like a house for giants!' cried Ollie, running into the room and throwing himself on to the sofa.

Lara could see what he meant. The room was easily big enough for a game of five-a-side football, including spectators. The sofas were twice as big as their sofas at home, and the carpet was twice as thick.

'This is the life,' Mr Cook sighed, sinking

into an armchair and putting his feet up on the footstool.

'Beautiful,' Mrs Cook murmured, stroking the polished surface of an oak dining table.

'Are these for us?' asked Sophie, pointing to two huge bowls full of sweets and chocolates.

'That's right,' said Mr Cartwright.

Spud's eyes lit up. 'My favourites!' he drooled, peering into the bowls.

'Which ones?' asked Star.

'All of them!' yapped Spud.

Ollie stopped running around the room just long enough to grab a handful of toffees.

'There's a bowl of lovely fruit as well, see?' said Mrs Cook, without much hope.

'Excuse me, Mr Cartwright. There are no beds. Where do we sleep?' asked Sophie.

'This is a suite, Sophie,' Mr Cartwright explained. 'The bedrooms are behind those doors.'

'There's more? Wow!' Sophie shot off with Ollie, Spud and Star to explore.

'Slow down!' shouted Mrs Cook.

'Slow down!' woofed Lara, at the same time.

'What do you think of the Wizard's Suite, Ben?' asked Mr Cartwright.

'It's amazing.'

Mr Cartwright smiled. 'You haven't seen the best bit yet.' He pressed a button and the curtains drew back to reveal a wall of windows. The Enchanted Towers Theme Park was spread out below them.

'You can see everything from here!' cried Ben, with such excitement that the others ran back from the bedrooms to see what all the fuss was about.

'Yes. We're nearly at the top of the hotel,' explained Mr Cartwright. 'Only the Penthouse is higher; that's where Summer Rayne will be staying tomorrow. Now, look over at the forest, Ben. What can you see?'

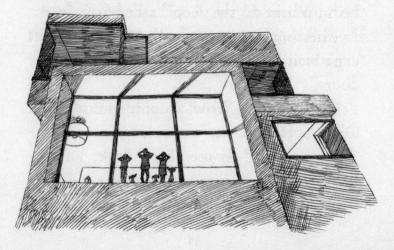

Ben looked where Mr Cartwright was pointing. He could see something coiling and twisting through the treetops. 'Is that Storm Spell?'

'Yes.'

Ben beamed with pride.

'Everything will be ready for our big Sunday launch,' said Mr Cartwright. 'The Enchanted Towers team have been hard at work painting "Storm Spell" on to the ride entrance and on the sides of all the carriages. Now, I'll leave you all to get some sleep. You need to be in the hotel lobby at nine in the morning. Princess Pretty will meet you there and take you across to the theme park.'

Ben turned back to the windows as the door closed behind Mr Cartwright. 'Storm-Spell,' he murmured, 'the world's fastest, scariest, twistiest and most stomach-churning ride! I can't wait for a go!'

Princess Pretty glared up at the Enchanted Towers Hotel. The lights were on in the Wizard's Suite on the tenth floor, but the Penthouse above it was in darkness.

'What are you looking at?' Darren asked.

'Summer Rayne will be staying in that Penthouse tomorrow night. It should be me up there, getting the star treatment!' Princess Pretty snarled. 'Come on, Darren. Now the park is closed for the night, our real work can begin.'

Darren sighed. They were part of a straggling line of fairies, wizards, goblins and witches, all making their way to the staff locker rooms to change out of their costumes. The others were all laughing and joking together; they loved their jobs at the park and thought Mr Cartwright was a good boss to work for. Suddenly Darren wished he was with them instead of with Princess Pretty.

'Darren?' whispered Princess Pretty, squeezing his hand. 'You are going to help me, aren't you?'

'Of course,' said Darren guiltily, bending to kiss her lovely face. How could he have thought about leaving her on her own?

'Snap out of it and get a move on, then!' growled Princess Pretty, yanking her hand away and stalking off.

Darren followed Princess Pretty into the back of the theatre building. Everyone was heading for the staff locker rooms at the end of the corridor but, after a quick glance around to check that nobody was watching them, Princess Pretty and Darren slipped through another door into the theatre itself. Princess Pretty hurried down into the orchestra pit, slid back one of the wooden panels edging the stage and stepped through. Darren took off his troll head and pushed back his floppy brown hair, which immediately flopped forward again. With his sad brown eyes and his droopy mouth, he looked like an unhappy spaniel. He bent his head and followed Princess Pretty under the stage into a low-ceilinged space the size of a large cupboard.

Princess Pretty slid the wooden panel back into place behind them and then switched on a torch hanging from a beam. One wall of her secret den was covered with newspaper clippings and photos of Summer Rayne. In all the images Summer's face had been scratched out or torn away.

Darren leant in to study one photograph more closely. It showed the cast of a musical. Summer Rayne, the star of the show, was at the front of the photograph, but Darren was focusing on the dark-haired girl in the back row of the chorus. It was Princess Pretty. 'Princess, why didn't you want Mr Cartwright to know that you and Summer had been in a musical together?'

'I'm planning to get my revenge on her, Darren! Best to keep a low profile.'

'But – won't *she* recognize you?'

'I doubt it. I was only a chorus girl, and it was years ago. Put these on,' Princess Pretty ordered, flinging a black tracksuit and beanie hat at Darren. 'We don't want to be seen out there.'

Darren frowned. 'Tell me again, Princess.

How did Summer Rayne steal you of going to Hollywood?'

Princess Pretty sighed impatiently as she smeared black camouflage paint across her face. 'I should've been the star of that musical, not her!' she hissed. 'I auditioned for the part – and the director loved my voice. He raised his eyebrows after my song and said, "Well, I've never heard anything quite like that before." I knew then the part was mine!'

Princess Pretty smiled at the memory and then glowered at the wall of photographs. 'Then Summer Rayne did *her* audition – and she got the part! She must've said something about me to the director; it's the only explanation. Anyway, a talent scout saw her in the show and, next thing I knew, *she* was off to Hollywood instead of me!'

Darren opened his mouth to say, 'Perhaps Summer Rayne was just the better singer?', but he couldn't make the words come out. Instead, he said, 'So what's the plan?'

'See that little dog she's always carrying around in her handbag?' said Princess, pointing all of photographs. 'The one that looks like a rat?'

'The chihuahua?'

'She loves that dog,' said Princess. 'So we're going to take it away from her.'

'D-dog-napping?' stammered Darren. 'How?'

Princess Pretty grabbed a hammer from the corner of her den and threw it across to him. 'Time to do some breaking and entering,' she said.

6. No Happy Endings

The security guard checked the gate at the entrance to the new Storm Spell ride. He yanked the chain to check it was secure. The man heard a rustling in the bushes and shone his torch in the direction of the noise.

The two black shadows crouched, their breath held as they heard footsteps crunching their way. A beam of light passed over them and they breathed a sigh of relief as the guard went on his way, whistling softly.

'Phew! That was close,' Darren whispered. 'Maybe we should just give up and go home.'

'Don't be silly!' hissed Princess Pretty. 'We're past the most dangerous bit now. The security guards don't patrol in the forest. Follow me!'

They slipped away under the trees and Princess Pretty led Darren deeper and deeper into the forest. With their black clothes and camouflaged faces, only the whites of their eyes gleamed in the moonlight as they crept from tree to tree. Finally, Princess Pretty stopped in front of a thick clump of bushes.

'Here,' she said. 'Put these gloves on and open the container.'

Darren shone his torch at the container they'd just stolen from a locked shed. 'Sulphuric acid!' he exclaimed. He glanced at Princess. 'We're not going to . . . you know?'

'No, Prince Pushover. We are not going to kill the dog. We're just going to kidnap it.'

'And how do we do that?'

'We use our pick-pocketing technique. When Summer's looking the other way, I yank the little rat – I mean dog – out of her handbag. I pass it back to you, and you drop it through the mouth of your troll head and into the secret pouch. Got that?'

Darren nodded. 'Then what?'

'Then we send Summer Rayne a ransom note.'

'And she gets her dog back?' asked Darren hopefully.

'Of course! Summer Rayne pays the ransom, gets her dog back and I get enough money to go to Hollywood and become a star! Happy endings all round.'

'That's all right, then!' said Darren. 'So why the acid?'

'It's not acid,' lied Princess Pretty. 'Someone's put it in the wrong container. It's special paint. And I want you to paint the metal leg of Storm Spell with it.'

Darren looked puzzled.

'Tomorrow is the launch, right? And we want it to look great, don't we?'

The part-time troll nodded. He loved Princess Pretty so very much.

'So get painting!' yelled his girlfriend. 'I've got some rope work to do over there. When I get back, I want this leg finished.'

There was a hissing sound as Darren applied the first lick of acid. Princess Pretty bounded off to complete her part of the evil plan. 'Darren is so stupid,' she chuckled. 'He'll believe anything! The first trip on the new rollercoaster will be the *only* trip! The acid will work its magic and when the carriage hurtles round the track, the leg will collapse and down will come Summer Rayne, Cook family and all.'

One thing was for sure: in this story there would be no happy ending for Summer Rayne or her dog. It was Princess Pretty who would live happily ever after.

7. Going Green

'Come on, Dad!' Ollie cried.

'Do I have to?' groaned Mr Cook.

The rest of the family were already sitting in one of the carriages of the Fee-Fi-Fo-Fum Beanstalk ride, but he was still hesitating on the platform.

'You promised you'd go on everything,' Sophie reminded him.

'That was six hours ago,' gulped Mr Cook. 'Since then we've been dropped from the top of Rapunzel's Tower six stomach-churning times, and we've taken five white-knuckle trips down the flume ride, not to mention all the other spinning, twisting, turning, whirling rides we've been on in between.'

'I know!' cried Mrs Cook. 'Hasn't it been

brilliant, dear? I haven't had this much fun in years!'

Mrs Cook's eyes were sparkling and her face was pink with excitement. In contrast, Mr Cook's face was nearly as green as the carriage in front of him.

'How bad is this going to be?' he asked, peering along the rollercoaster track.

Darren leant forward in his seat. He was wearing his troll costume, so his voice was muffled. 'Actually, Mr Cook, the corkscrew bit is pretty awful,' he said.

'Pardon?' said Mr Cook.

'He said, you'll be fine, Mr Cook!' Princess Pretty lied. 'It's really very slow and gentle.'

'Well . . . If you say so,' said Mr Cook.

'Don't listen to her!' barked Lara, scowling at Princess Pretty from the viewing platform. 'I wouldn't trust her as far as I could throw her!'

But Mr Cook had already climbed into the seat beside Mrs Cook and was allowing the attendant to fasten him in. 'Don't look so worried, Lara. I'll be fine as long as it doesn't go too fa*AAAGGGHHH*!'

Mr Cook's screams faded into the distance

as the carriage shot round a bend in the track at breakneck speed.

'The more I see of Princess Pretty, the less I like her,' Lara growled.

'Poor Mr Cook,' woofed Star. 'He isn't enjoying himself much, is he?'

'He's not the only one,' Spud grumbled. 'We've spent the whole day looking for pick-pockets and we haven't caught a single one.'

'Let's do another search while we're waiting for the Cooks,' woofed Lara.

'We might be lucky this time,' yapped Star.

'Do we have to? My paws are sore!' whined Spud.

'Spy Dogs do their job, even when their paws are sore,' said Lara firmly. 'Cameras on, pups.'

Lara, Spud and Star gave their heart lockets a twist with their front paws and then plunged back into the crowd. It was the first Saturday of the summer holidays and the Enchanted Towers Theme Park was packed. Suddenly a man ran past them clutching a handbag under his arm.

'Bag-snatcher!' Star yapped. 'After him!'

Lara, Spud and Star raced after the man. He

was dodging and weaving through the crowds as fast as he could, but they were faster.

'We're gaining on him!' panted Lara. 'When we reach him, I'll grab the bag –'

'And I'll bite his bum!' yapped Spud.

'No! You two stay back!' barked Lara, pushing herself to run faster.

'Look out, Ma!' yelled Star. 'He's stopped!'

Lara tried to slow down, but she tripped over her own paws and ended up in an ungainly heap at the bag-snatcher's feet.

How embarrassing, she thought, scrambling up again and trying to pretend nothing had happened.

'Hello, old girl,' said the man, smiling down at her. 'Where did you come from?'

'Less of the "old", Mr Bag-snatcher!' snarled Lara. 'Hand it over!'

But the man was already handing over the handbag to a very grateful woman. 'You left it on the bench back there,' he said. 'I'm so glad I managed to catch you.'

Oops! He's not snatching a bag: he's returning it!

Lara ducked her head and sneaked back to Spud and Star.

'Did you enjoy your trip, Ma?' asked Star innocently.

Spud let out a snort of laughter. 'This is going straight on YouTube,' he yapped, pointing to his camera locket.

Lara gave Spud a hard stare.

'Um . . . I mean it *would* go on YouTube, if you weren't a Spy Dog on an undercover mission,' said Spud hastily.

'What do we do now?' asked Star. 'Keep looking for pick-pockets?'

'I can't see the point,' Lara huffed. 'All the visitors are behaving far too well today. Come on. The Fee-Fi-Fo-Fum ride is coming back. I can hear Mr Cook screaming.'

The carriages were just pulling in when Lara, Spud and Star trotted up to the platform.

'Oh dear,' Lara woofed, watching Mr Cook stagger off the ride. 'He's gone even greener!'

'Are you all right, dear?' asked Mrs Cook.

'Blurp.' A look of panic crept into Mr Cook's eyes.

'Pardon?'

'Blaarp.' He clapped a hand over his mouth and looked wildly about him. A man was walking past holding a jumbo-sized carton of popcorn. Mr Cook snatched the carton and stuck his face into it.

'*Blearghh!*'

Spud pulled a face. *Yuck! Even I wouldn't fancy that flavour popcorn!*

'Sorry,' Mr Cook said, wiping his mouth with a shaky hand. 'Let me buy you some more.'

'No thanks,' said the man, hurrying away. 'I've just lost my appetite.'

'Let's do that again!' cried Ollie.

'Absolutely not. I'm choosing the next ride,' said Mr Cook. 'Something nice and gentle. Look. Over there. That's just the job.' He pointed at the Goblin Mine Ghost Train across the street.

'But that goes really slowly, Dad,' said Sophie.

'Exactly,' said Mr Cook, wiping the sweat from his brow.

'And there are no ups and downs,' added Ollie.

'Precisely,' said Mr Cook, turning a little less green.

'All you do is trundle around in the dark and wait for stuff to jump out at you,' said Ben.

'Hopefully,' said Mr Cook.

'Remember that ghost ride we went on when we were courting, dear?' said Mrs Cook, cuddling up to him.

'Absolutely,' smiled Mr Cook, putting his arm round her.

'Look!' said Princess Pretty, her eyes glittering darkly as she watched a helicopter flying low overhead. 'That's the lovely Summer Rayne arriving. Let's go and meet her, shall we?'

Ben and Ollie exchanged a disgusted glance. They didn't want to waste a minute of their precious Enchanted Towers day pass, especially if it meant having to talk politely to some girl they had never met before. Sophie, on the other hand, was hugging herself with excitement.

'I can't believe I'm going to meet Summer Rayne!' she said as Princess Pretty guided them towards the theatre. 'I suppose this is just another day's work for her, though.'

'Oh, I don't know,' said Princess Pretty. 'I think Summer Rayne is going to have a very exciting time with us!'

8. Cupcake

'I think Storm Spell is such a brilliant name!' said Summer Rayne, smiling at Ben. 'The "Storm" part captures the speed and danger of the ride, and the "Spell" part captures the magic of Enchanted Towers. Well done, Ben.'

Ben blushed deeply and mumbled his thanks.

'Look!' yapped Spud. 'Even his ears have gone red!'

'I'm not surprised,' woofed Lara. 'She really is very pretty.'

'Huh!' Spud snorted. 'You won't find me going soft like that over some girl!'

They were in Summer Rayne's dressing room. Summer, Mr Cartwright and the Cook family were clustered together on three sofas,

Princess Pretty and her Troll Prince were standing behind them, and Lara, Spud and Star were sitting on the floor.

'She seems really nice,' woofed Lara, watching Summer laugh and chat with the Cooks. 'Kind and friendly, and not at all spoiled.'

'Ben certainly seems to think so,' giggled Star. 'Just think! Five minutes ago, he didn't even want to meet her. Now look at him!'

Ben was leaning towards Summer Rayne with a goofy smile on his face, totally ignoring Ollie, who was shooting betrayed glances his way.

'Yeuch! What's happened to him?' yapped Spud. 'Everyone knows you don't waste time on girls – unless she's your sister, of course!' he added hastily, dodging Star's paw.

'What lovely dogs!' cried Summer Rayne. 'What are their names?'

'Lara, Spud and Star,' said Ben.

Summer reached into the big shoulder bag on the sofa beside her. 'Lara, Spud and Star,' she said, bringing her hand out of the bag, 'meet my darling little dog, Cupcake.'

Sitting in Summer's hand was a tiny chihuahua. She blinked her round, chocolate-brown eyes and looked down her titchy nose at them.

'Hello, Cupcake,' woofed Lara.

'How dare you talk to me!' squeaked Cupcake. 'You're not even pedigree!'

'Why don't you four get to know one another while we're chatting?' said Summer, lowering her hand.

Cupcake's round eyes grew even rounder. 'Stop!' she squeaked. 'Don't put me down here with the mongrels! Who knows what diseases they have! Oh! Oh no! Now I'm on the dirty floor! Unbelievable!'

Cupcake stood, balancing on her tiny toes, so that she touched as little of the floor as possible.

One flick of my paw and she'd topple right over, thought Lara. It was very tempting, but Cupcake was trembling and her big brown eyes looked close to tears. Lara decided to have another go at being friendly.

'I like your outfit,' she said, waving her paw at the pink feathered waistcoat Cupcake was wearing.

'And what would you know about fashion, you big, hairy, smelly lump?' demanded Cupcake. 'FYI,' she added, pointing at the bullet-hole in Lara's sticky-up ear, 'piercings are *so* last year.'

'FYI?' said Lara, looking to Star for help. 'What does that mean?'

'Oh! Talk to the paw,' squeaked Cupcake, holding up her front leg. 'Cos I ain't listening!'

'Don't you talk to my mum like that!' snapped Star, her hackles rising. 'She's a famous Spy Dog!'

'Spy Dog, Shmy Dog,' yawned Cupcake, examining her pink-painted claws. 'Give me your locket.'

'Excuse me?' gasped Star.

'Your pink locket,' squeaked Cupcake. 'It's pretty. And it, like, totally goes with my outfit. Give it to me.'

'Get lost, shrimp!' snarled Star.

'Give me yours, then,' ordered Cupcake, turning to Lara.

'Why?'

'Because I want it! And I always get what I ask for.'

'Right now, you're asking for a poke in the eye! Don't tempt me!' growled Lara.

'It'll have to be yours, then,' squeaked Cupcake, turning to Spud, who had been strangely silent so far.

'Yeah, sure, you can have it,' said Spud, pressing the release stud on his collar. 'I didn't like it anyway.'

'Spud! What are you doing?' woofed Lara and Star as Spud pushed Professor Cortex's expensive gadget across the floor to Cupcake.

Spud didn't answer. He was too busy gazing at Cupcake with a goofy smile on his face.

'Oh, look!' cried Summer Rayne. 'Spud has just given Cupcake a present. How sweet is that?' She clipped Spud's locket on to Cupcake's collar and then scooped her up. 'There. You look lovely!'

'Of course,' sighed Cupcake. 'I always do.'

'Ms Rayne, would you like to say hello to some of your fans before the show?' asked Mr Cartwright.

'That would be lovely,' said Summer,

slipping Cupcake back into her shoulder bag and standing up.

Lara and Star were still gazing at Spud in astonishment, so they didn't notice Princess Pretty staring greedily at Cupcake.

'You said we'd never catch you going soft over some girl!' hissed Star, digging Spud in the ribs as they followed everyone out of the dressing room.

Spud shook his head as though he was emerging from a trance. 'Don't know what came over me,' he muttered, giving his sister a shamefaced look. 'She must've poisoned me with something.'

Star nodded seriously. 'You know what I think? I think she gave you a very strong dose of BBE.'

'BBE? What does that stand for?' yapped Spud, looking worried.

'Big brown eyes,' barked Star, trotting after Lara.

'Huh! Very funny,' yapped Spud, catching up.

'We need to get that locket back,' woofed Lara. 'It wasn't yours to give, Spud. It belongs to Professor Cortex.'

'Leave this to me, Ma,' growled Spud.

He caught up with Summer Rayne and barked at the shoulder bag until Cupcake poked her head over the top.

'Yes, mongrel?'

'Can I have my locket back?'

'It's mine now. You gave it to me.'

'That was a mistake,' yapped Spud. 'I need it —'

'I need it more,' interrupted Cupcake. 'I am the most photographed dog in the world! I always have to look my best. It's a lot of pressure.'

'Pressure? Don't be daft,' yapped Spud.

Just then, Mr Cartwright pushed open the theatre doors and ushered Summer Rayne outside into an explosion of screams and camera flashes. Spud staggered back, stunned by the noise and the light, but Summer kept walking, waving and smiling, and Cupcake struck a pose, turning this way and that for the cameras. Princess Pretty and her Troll Prince followed close behind.

Hmm. She might just have a point about the pressure, Spud admitted, blinking the camera flashes away.

'Keep up!' woofed Lara. She plunged into the crowd, followed by Spud and Star. By the time they reached Summer Rayne, she had stopped walking and was cheerfully signing autographs. She had pushed her shoulder bag round behind her back to keep Cupcake safely out of the way.

'What do we do now, Ma?' yapped Star.

'We stay close and watch for our chance to get that locket back,' woofed Lara.

But the chance never came. Summer Rayne signed autographs until Mr Cartwright held up his hands and called a halt. 'That's all, folks. See you at the show tonight.'

The autograph-hunters fell back and Summer brought her shoulder bag round to the front again. She looked inside and then gave a horrified scream. 'Cupcake! My Cupcake's gone!'

'What!' gasped Mr Cartwright. 'Well, I'm sure she can't have gone far; she's only got little legs.'

'No, you don't understand!' Summer wailed. 'Cupcake would never run away. Someone's stolen her right out of my bag!'

Lara turned cold with shock and then hot

with shame. The pick-pocket she had been searching for all day had struck again right under her nose and she hadn't noticed a thing! *How did I miss that? I was staring right at Summer Rayne!* She could hear Professor Cortex's voice in her head. 'Spy Dogs don't just stare, GM451; Spy Dogs *observe*.'

Lara shook herself and turned to her pups. 'Full Cupcake alert! Star, you go left. Spud, you go right. I'll go straight ahead. We'll see if we can sniff her out.'

They set off, noses to the ground, but the crowd were all searching for Cupcake too, getting in the way and stomping all over any possible scent trails. Lara glanced across at Mr Cartwright, hoping he might take control, but he was standing beside a weeping Summer, gazing helplessly at the chaos all around him.

That was when Mum and Dad Cook sprang into action. Lara felt a surge of pride as she watched them. *I adopted the right family*, she thought. *No doubt about it!*

Mrs Cook put her arm round Summer, produced the clean, white hankie she always seemed to carry and told the superstar that crying wouldn't help to find Cupcake.

Mr Cook pushed his way into the centre of the crowd, drew himself up to his full height and yelled, 'STOP!'

And the whole crowd stopped.

Just for a second, Mr Cook had everyone's full attention. He didn't hesitate. He knew exactly what to do next because he was a dad! Years of hunting for lost hamsters, lost pet snakes and lost children had prepared him for just this moment.

'Stay absolutely still!' he ordered.

The crowd froze.

'Good. Now, everyone turn full circle on the spot. If you see any sign of Cupcake, raise your hand!'

The crowd obeyed but, when they had finished turning in a circle, nobody raised a hand. Cupcake had disappeared.

'Thank you,' said Mr Cook. 'I think it's time to search the rest of the park. I'm dividing you into four search groups.' He held out his arm and marked off each group. 'North, south, east and west. If anyone finds Cupcake, please bring her straight here to the theatre, where Summer and Mr Cartwright will be waiting.'

Hearing his name seemed to shake Mr Cartwright back into action. 'Yes!' he cried. 'And if – I mean when – Cupcake is returned, I will announce it over the park's PA system and call off the search.'

'Thank you, Mr Cartwright,' said Mr Cook. 'Off you go, everyone – and good luck!'

The crowd gave Mr Cook a cheer and then scattered to search the park.

'Can we search too, Dad?' asked Ben.

'As long as you stay together,' said Mr Cook.

'Lara, will you keep an eye on them?' asked Mrs Cook.

'Of course,' woofed Lara, giving Mrs Cook a nod. 'Come on, pups! We can watch the children and look for Cupcake at the same time.'

Spud and Star ran after Ben, Sophie and Ollie. Lara was about to follow, but something made her look back. Mrs Cook was leading Summer Rayne into the theatre, followed by Mr Cook and Mr Cartwright. Princess Pretty and her Troll Prince were at the back of the sad little group.

Lara frowned. *Except Princess Pretty doesn't look at all sad*, she thought.

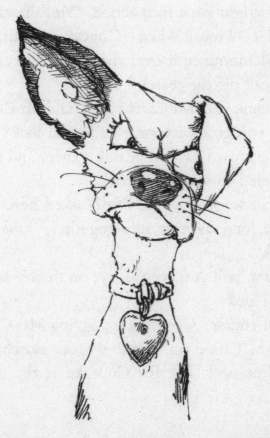

Look at the way she's bouncing along, swinging her arms and – her hand is bleeding! Could that be a dog bite? Could she have stolen Cupcake? But, if she did, where is Cupcake now? Princess Pretty didn't have time to hide her . . .

The Cook children, and her pups, were already far down the street. Lara hesitated, looking between them and Princess Pretty. *I'll have to stay with the children*, she thought. *I made a promise to Mrs Cook. But be warned, Princess Pretty, I'll be back. You're the very next thing on my list!*

9. The Show Must Go On

Lara kept an ear cocked for an announcement that Cupcake had been found, but the announcement never came, and so they kept searching the park right up to the time when Summer Rayne's show was due to start.

'It's no good,' sighed Star as they trailed back to the theatre behind Ben, Sophie and Ollie. 'Cupcake seems to have vanished into thin air!'

'And I think I might know who made her vanish,' Lara admitted. 'But I just can't figure out how!'

She told Spud and Star about the blood on Princess Pretty's hand.

'Girls!' growled Spud. 'Nothing but trouble! Why don't we tell Mr Cartwright?'

'Because we don't have a scrap of evidence,' woofed Lara.

'What about the blood?' asked Star.

Lara shook her head. 'A scratched hand doesn't prove anything. No, I think it's up to us to investigate Princess Pretty ourselves.'

'Yay! Spy Dogs to the rescue!' yapped Spud. 'Come on! Let's go find her!'

But when they reached the theatre and hurried up to the VIP box where Mr and Mrs Cook were waiting for them, there was no sign of Princess Pretty or her Troll Prince.

'How about this for special treatment?' said Mr Cook, pointing out the leather armchairs and velvet curtains. 'Pity it's not in happier circumstances.'

Once Ben, Sophie and Ollie were sitting down, Lara pointed to the remaining two empty armchairs and then raised her eyebrows questioningly. *Where's Princess Pretty?*

'Of course you can sit down, Lara,' said Mr Cook. 'You don't need to ask.'

Lara shook her head. *Thanks, but no thanks. I'm a bit busy being a Spy Dog.*

'He's not getting it, Ma,' said Star. 'Try again.'

Lara held up imaginary skirts and gave a curtsy before raising a paw to her eyes and pretending to search the box. *Princess Pretty. Where is she?*

'Oh! "I'm a little teapot, short and stout"?' guessed Mrs Cook.

Lara slapped a paw to her forehead. *I'm not playing charades! This is serious!*

'She's asking where Princess Pretty is,' said Ollie.

Lara sent him a grateful look. *Thank you, Ollie.*

'Oh! I see!' said Mr Cook. 'She's gone home, Lara. She and her troll finished work at five o'clock. She'll be back bright and early tomorrow morning, ready for the launch of Storm Spell.'

'Oh, look! The curtain's going up!' said Mrs Cook. 'Summer's a brave girl. She told me the show must go on. Out of the way, Lara. You're blocking my view.'

Lara gave up. She climbed on to the remaining leather armchair and settled down for a good think. *I can do* The Times *crossword in record time, so I'm sure I can figure out how Princess Pretty managed to steal Cupcake in full view of two hundred people and three Spy Dogs!*

A single spotlight shone down on to the stage. Summer Rayne was standing there, head bowed, holding her empty shoulder bag. The audience rose up from their seats and clapped and clapped. Summer waited quietly until they sat down again and silence descended on the theatre.

'Thank you,' she said. 'Before I begin, I'd like to offer a reward for the return of my dog, Cupcake. I will pay ten thousand pounds to the person who brings her back to me safe and well.'

An excited buzz went round the theatre and some audience members got out their mobile phones and started texting. The word would spread fast.

'And now,' said Summer, carefully placing the empty shoulder bag at the front of the stage and lifting the microphone from its stand, 'I'd like to sing for you – and for Cupcake, wherever she is.'

'She's a lot closer than you think, Summer Rayne,' sneered Princess Pretty, from her lair beneath the stage. 'Aren't you, you little rat?' Princess kicked the plastic travel crate at her feet and a muffled whimper came from behind the grille.

'Did you have to tie her paws together and wrap that elastic band round her muzzle?' said Darren, peering in at Cupcake.

Princess Pretty pointed to the plaster on her hand. 'I'm not giving her another chance to sink her teeth into me! Besides, we don't

want her barking and giving us away, do we? Now, be quiet while I finish this ransom note. There's enough noise to put up with already, what with that awful singing right above my head!' Princess cut one last word from the newspaper with her scissors and then stuck it to a sheet of paper. 'Ten thousand pounds?' she muttered as she worked. 'That's peanuts! She'll have to fork out a lot more than that before I'm finished. There!' she said, holding up the sheet for Darren to see.

To get Cupcake back, come to the theatre at 9.00 tomorrow morning and leave £100,000 in a backpack on the stage. Don't call the police. Come alone, or you will never see your dog again. When Storm Spell is launched, make sure you are on it. If the launch is delayed, you will never see your dog again. If you do everything I say, you and Cupcake will meet again at the end of the ride.

Darren nodded miserably. 'As long as they do meet again.'

Oh, there's no doubt about that, thought

Princess Pretty, imagining Summer's screams as her Storm Spell carriage crashed into the forest. *In fact, I think their meeting will make quite an impact. On the ground!*

'But how?' said Darren stubbornly. 'How do we reunite them?'

'You, Darren, get to ride on Storm Spell with Summer Rayne, you lucky boy! Don't wear your troll costume, though; it'll make you too big to fit into the harness. While you're keeping an eye on Summer, I'll make sure that Cupcake is ready and waiting for her at the other end.'

Bye-bye, Darren, she thought. *You're no use to me any more. I'm off to Hollywood on my own!*

'But aren't you supposed to be on the launch ride too?' asked Darren.

'You can tell them I'm too scared to go on it, cos I'm only a girly-girl,' said Princess Pretty, putting on a baby voice.

Darren nodded. 'What happens now?' he asked, watching Princess Pretty fold the ransom note and put it in an envelope.

'Once the show's over and the park is empty, I'll take Cupcake to a little hideaway in the forest.'

'And then will you untie her and take the elastic band off her muzzle?'

'If you insist,' sighed Princess Pretty. 'No one will hear the little rat way out there. While I'm hiding Cupcake, you deliver the ransom note to the hotel.'

'How do I do it without being seen?'

'Don't worry about that, Darren. I have a plan. After that, we sneak back here and wait for my money to arrive. Simple!'

Lara was still deep in thought when Summer Rayne's show came to an end, but she was no nearer to solving the puzzle.

When the applause finally stopped, Mr Cook picked up a sleeping Ollie and held him against his shoulder, and Mrs Cook put her arm round a yawning Sophie.

'Coming, Lara?' asked Ben. 'We're heading back to the hotel.'

Lara gave him an affectionate lick and then raised her paw. *We'll be along in a minute.*

Ben shuffled off after his mum and dad, rubbing his eyes tiredly. It had been a long day.

'Come on, pups,' woofed Lara.

'Where to, Ma?' asked Star, stifling a yawn

as she jumped down from the armchair she was sharing with Spud.

'Back to the place where Cupcake went missing. Time for a crime scene investigation.'

'Can it be a quick investigation?' Spud muttered, snuggling down in the warm spot Star had just left.

'Very quick,' said Lara, feeling guilty. It had been a long day for her pups too.

Outside the theatre, they waited quietly in a shadowy alley that ran down the side of the building. The stream of people leaving the theatre died away to a trickle and then stopped altogether. The theatre lights went out one by one until, finally, the building was in darkness.

Good, thought Lara. *Everyone's gone home. Now we can investigate in peace.* 'Ready, pups?'

'Ready,' whispered Star.

'Zzzz . . .' snored Spud.

Lara and Star looked round. Spud had gone to sleep standing up. He was leaning against a door with his chin resting on the doorstep.

'Spud!' hissed Star.

Spud jerked awake. 'I didn't eat the last biscuit!'

'Come on,' Lara chuckled, nudging him into an upright position.

They had taken only a few steps away from the door when an eerie *crreeaak* came from the shadows behind them. Spud and Star froze in place, their eyes wide.

Crreeeaaakkk . . .

Lara looked over her shoulder. The door Spud had been sleeping against only a second ago was slowly opening! Someone, or something, was coming out from under the stage.

10. Moonlit Chase

'Run!' Lara hissed.

Spud and Star needed no second telling. They raced away from the opening door as fast as their short legs would go. Lara ran behind her pups, hoping they wouldn't trip over their own paws. Just as they reached the front of the theatre, Lara risked a glance back. The door was now fully open and a dark shape was stepping down into the alley.

Lara threw herself round the corner after Spud and Star. 'Quick! Behind that hedge!'

They leapt over a low hedge and then flattened themselves to the ground. Lara could hear two pairs of soft footsteps walking down the alley towards them. She raised her head so that just her eyes and her sticky-up ear were above the top of the hedge. Two people dressed in black came out of the alley. One was very tall and the other was small and slim. The smaller person was leading the way and the tall one was carrying a small plastic box with a grille on the front.

'Princess Pretty and her troll,' breathed Lara.

'How do you know?' whispered Star. 'They both have camouflage paint on their faces and black beanie hats over their hair.'

'Hurry up, Darren!' snapped the small figure. 'I haven't got all night!'

'Yep, that's Princess Potty, all right,' growled Spud.

'So, the troll's in on it too,' Lara mused. 'I think I'm beginning to see how they stole Cupcake without anyone noticing.'

'Speaking of Cupcake,' whispered Star, sniffing the air. 'She's in that cage. Where are they taking her?'

'Let's find out, shall we?' said Lara.

They followed Princess Pretty and Darren like three shadows, dodging between waste bins, closed ice-cream stalls and empty ticket kiosks until they came to a big open square with nothing to hide behind.

'What do we do now?' whispered Star as

they watched Princess Pretty and Darren hurry away across the square. 'If we wait until they're out of sight before we follow them, we might lose them!'

'They haven't looked back once,' said Spud. 'Shall we risk it, Ma?'

Princess Pretty and Darren were halfway across now. Lara made a decision. 'Let's go for it!'

They set off, running silently and keeping low to the ground. They had reached the centre of the square, with nowhere to hide, when Cupcake spotted them through the grille of the travel crate. She began struggling against her bonds and letting out muffled squeaks of excitement.

'What's up with the rat?' Princess Pretty demanded.

'Dunno,' said Darren, lifting the crate and peering inside. Cupcake's round brown eyes were nearly popping out of her head. She was staring at something behind him. Darren looked over his shoulder. 'Princess! We're being followed!'

'Oops,' woofed Lara, stopping dead with one paw in the air.

'What!' Princess Pretty whirled round. 'Oh, it's only those stupid dogs!'

'Less of the stupid, Princess Potty!' growled Spud.

'But why are they following us?' whined Darren guiltily. 'Do you think they know what we're up to?'

'Of course not. They've just picked up Cupcake's scent, that's all. Still, we'd better get rid of them.' Princess Pretty picked up a stone and threw it as hard as she could. It hit Star on the nose, making her yelp.

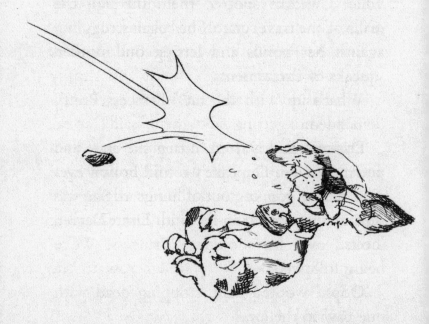

'Star!' woofed Lara. 'Are you all right?'

'That stung a bit,' said Star bravely, rubbing her nose.

'You're for it now!' yapped Spud. 'Nobody hits my sister!'

Spud, Lara and Star lined up shoulder to shoulder and stalked forward, growling deep in their throats.

Princess Pretty picked up another stone.

'Don't!' pleaded Darren. 'They're only dogs.'

'Yes, but where dogs go, humans might follow. We can't have them leading people to Cupcake; that'll ruin all my plans.'

Princess Pretty threw the second stone at Lara, but she was ready for it and simply stepped aside.

'That's not getting rid of them,' said Darren.

Princess Pretty looked around and then broke into a smile. 'But this will! Follow me!' She ran to one of the buildings edging the square and ducked inside with Darren at her heels.

Lara, Spud and Star raced across to the building.

'Haunted House,' read Spud, a shiver

working its way down his spine. 'I don't like g . . . g . . . ghosts.'

'Come on, silly,' woofed Star, nosing her way through the front door. 'They're not real. There's no such thing as . . .' Star shot out of the Haunted House with her tail between her legs. Lara caught her by the collar and lifted her off the ground, her tiny legs still running.

Spud was hiding his face in his mum's furry tum.

'OK, you two,' gulped Lara. 'You stand guard here and check Pretty and the troll don't escape through this door. And I'll be the brave one who follows them through the Haunted House.'

Spud peered out of her fur and nodded. Star was shaking, her fur standing on end. Lara was a little unnerved. *Whatever is beyond the front door must be pretty spooky*, she thought. *But a Spy Dog sometimes has to venture into the unknown! The Prof always says 'fortune favours the brave'.*

Lara tiptoed through the entrance, her doggie eyes adjusting to the blackness. She nearly jumped out of her skin as a laughing clown leered at her and she felt a spider run along her back. *It's not real*, she kept thinking to herself. *It's all in the mind. And besides, the baddies are getting away. I must get a move on!*

Lara crept round the next corner. *Not real. Not real.* She was half expecting Darren to jump out at her with a weapon so when Dracula leapt out of a grave, she karate-chopped him and his head fell off. His laugh was cut short and his red eyes went out. *Whoops*, thought Lara. *Sorry, Count D! Instincts and adrenaline have taken over.*

She edged her way through several of the Haunted House rooms. *Not real. Not real.* The kitchen had a scary chef holding a big meat cleaver. *And look at all that blood on his apron*, thought Lara. *I wouldn't want a meal prepared by him!*

Someone's watching me, she thought as she tiptoed through the sparsely lit living room. Lara looked up and the portraits had eyes. She shivered and her hackles were on full alert. She put her nose to the ground, sniffing for clues. Her eyes were everywhere. Her body was twitching, ready for a fight. She nosed her way through a graveyard, past some coffins and a warty-nosed hag. The final corridor was full of evil laughter and a tangle of cobwebs. Lara battled on and was glad to see an exit sign. She burst out into the cool night air with a sense of relief. *And that's what humans do for fun? Amazing!*

No sign of the baddies. Lara sprinted round to the front of the Haunted House where her pups were holding tightly to each other, their teeth chattering. They hugged their mum. 'Did you get 'em, Ma?' asked Spud.

Lara shook her head. 'No, son,' she woofed.

'They've escaped. Princess Pretty works here, remember? She knows these rides like the back of her hand.'

'She might have got away this time, Ma,' woofed Star through chattering teeth. 'But we'll get her next time.'

11. Imposters!

The dogs headed back to the hotel.

'Pups, I don't think we should tell anyone about Princess Pretty just yet,' Lara said as they rode up to the tenth floor in the lift.

'Why not?' asked Star. 'She's guilty of dog-napping and probably a whole host of other evil deeds too.'

'They should lock her up and throw away the key!' growled Spud.

'I agree,' said Lara. 'But if we have her arrested now, we may never find Cupcake.'

Spud and Star were silent, thinking about Cupcake all alone in a tiny plastic crate, slowly realizing that nobody was coming to rescue her. Finally, Star nodded. 'She's an annoying little madam, but she doesn't deserve that.'

'So, what do we do, Ma?' asked Spud.

'We keep tabs on her until she leads us to Cupcake.'

'Then it's prison for Princess Potty!' yapped Spud.

Back at the Wizard's Suite, Lara was surprised to find everyone still awake. Even more surprisingly, Summer Rayne was sitting on one of their big sofas, surrounded by tissues and looking very upset.

'There's been a ransom note, Lara,' Ben whispered, in answer to her enquiring look.

Who delivered it? Lara mimed writing a note and then handing it over to someone.

Ben nodded. 'It was a guy in a motorcycle helmet with a tinted glass visor. He gave it to the receptionist and left straight away.'

Clever, thought Lara. *No one saw his face. That must've been Princess Pretty's idea; Darren's not exactly the brightest button in the box.*

'Summer's determined to get Cupcake back, so she's following the instructions to the letter. She's having the ransom money helicoptered in from her personal bank account right now, ready for tomorrow. The note says she has to take the money to the theatre in a rucksack.'

'This is perfect!' Lara woofed quietly to Spud and Star. 'Now we know exactly where Princess Pretty will be tomorrow morning. We'll follow the ransom money. When Princess Pretty collects it, we'll stick to her like glue – and she'll lead us to Cupcake!'

The next morning, when Summer left the hotel disguised under a floppy sun hat and a pair of shades, the dogs followed her at a discreet distance. Summer went into the theatre alone, carrying the ransom money, and then came out again, empty-handed.

'So far so good,' muttered Lara, watching Summer slip quietly away into the crowd, unrecognized. 'Now we wait for Princess Pretty.'

They had just settled down behind a handy bush when the Enchanted Parks PA system crackled into life.

'All spare staff needed at the main entrance gates!' shouted Mr Cartwright. 'Repeat! All spare staff to the main entrance gates! Now!'

'He sounds desperate!' woofed Star. 'Should we go there or stay here?'

Lara scratched her head as she tried to

decide. *If we leave, we might miss Princess Pretty, but what if the trouble at the gates has something to do with Cupcake's dog-napping?*

'We could split up,' yapped Spud, eyeing a nearby donut stall. 'I'll stay here and do the slurp-out – I mean stake-out.'

'No,' woofed Lara. 'While there's a dog-napper on the loose, we stay together. Let's head for the main gate.'

'Spy Dogs straight into the action, as usual!' yapped Spud, bounding off in the direction of the gates with Star at his side. 'Good call, Ma!'

I hope so, thought Lara, racing after them. *Cupcake's life depends on it!*

'Where did they all come from?' gasped Star as they rounded a corner and the entrance gates came into view. A queue of people stretched from the turnstiles all the way back to the road on the other side of the car park, and every person in the queue had a dog with them.

Mr Cartwright was standing in front of the turnstiles with a line of Enchanted Park staff, blocking the way into the grounds. The queue was getting restless.

'This is Cupcake, and I claim my ten thousand pound reward!' shouted one man, holding up a scared-looking whippet.

'No! This is Cupcake and *I* claim the reward!' shouted another, brandishing a very young Dobermann pup.

'Calm down, everyone!' cried Mr Cartwright as the men squared up to one another, nose to nose, in the car park. 'You will all be seen! And if one of you has Cupcake, you will get your reward!'

In no time at all, Mr Cartwright had organized his staff into a double line, creating a channel curving from the turnstiles to a trestle table with a row of chairs behind it, then back down to the exit. By that time, Summer Rayne had arrived on the scene, with the Cook family.

'But there are so many of them!' cried Summer. 'I can't possibly check them all before the Storm Spell launch – and I have to be on that ride, on time!'

'Don't worry, Summer,' said Mr Cook. 'You don't need to stay for this. We'll do it for you. It'll be like the X Factor auditions – we'll whisk all these fortune-hunters past the table and straight back out of the exit! Lara, Spud, Star, you can help too.'

Mr Cartwright gently led Summer away

and then, for the next hour, they checked dog after dog, hoping one of them would be Cupcake.

'It's amazing what some people will do for money,' yapped Spud, gazing sympathetically at a shaved Yorkshire terrier with a pink bow tied round its bald head.

'Next!' shouted Ben, waving the terrier and its glowering owner towards the exit.

'Now that's just ridiculous!' woofed Lara as a man arrived at the table with a huge Great Dane in tow.

'This *is* Cupcake!' the owner insisted, patting the Great Dane on the head. 'Short hair, sticky-up ears, brown eyes, pink waist-coat. See?'

'But your dog is enormous,' sighed Mrs Cook.

'So?' said the owner.

'So, *this* dog is tiny,' said Mrs Cook, holding up a photograph of Cupcake.

The owner peered at the photograph. 'It could just be very far away.'

'Next!' bellowed Mr Cartwright.

'This is —'

'A CAT!' roared Ollie, giving the owner

such a fierce stare that she carried her cat away again without another word.

The chihuahuas were more difficult – some of them did look very like Cupcake – but Spud soon devised a test to weed them out. 'Can you tell me what I gave you yesterday?' he asked every chihuahua brought to the table.

'No idea, mate,' woofed one young male cheerfully. 'Can you tell me why my owner has suddenly started calling me Cupcake?'

'A kiss?' guessed a pretty female, making Spud blush.

'Chocolates?' said another, licking her lips.

'I wish,' slurped Spud, suddenly hungry. 'Next!'

When the last hopeful owner had been shown the exit, a short, sad silence fell over the group sitting at the table. Deep down, they had all been hoping that somewhere in among all those dogs – and cats – Cupcake would be found.

'Oh well,' said Mr Cartwright, getting to his feet. 'We'd better get going. It's nearly time for the launch of Storm Spell!'

'And we'd better get going too,' Lara

woofed to her pups. 'Back to the theatre, double-quick. Princess Pretty just might still be there!'

But when they sneaked into the empty theatre, the backpack of money had gone from the stage and there was no sign of Princess Pretty. Lara's shoulders slumped and she sat down heavily on one of the plush velvet theatre seats. *Looks like Princess Pretty got the better of me*, she thought.

'Look, Ma!' Star whispered, pointing towards the stage. 'One of those wooden panels on the front is loose! I wonder what's behind the gap.'

They crept through the orchestra pit and flattened themselves against the front of the stage, on each side of the gap left by the loose panel. Lara listened carefully and then, signalling to Spud and Star to stay where they were, she put her eye to the gap.

There was no movement in the gloom under the stage, so she carefully widened the gap by sliding the panel further back.

'Yikes!' she yelped, jumping backwards as a snarling, snaggle-toothed face emerged from the gloom.

'It's all right, Ma,' giggled Star. 'It's only Darren's troll head!'

The troll head was blocking the way in so, together, they pulled it and the rest of Darren's costume out into the orchestra pit. The body of the costume was all in one piece, with a set of braces inside to hold it on to the wearer's shoulders, but Lara was more interested in the head. She poked her nose inside and nodded in satisfaction when she saw the hidden pouch below the mouth. 'Thought so,' she said. 'That's how they stole Cupcake. Out of Summer's bag and straight into the troll's mouth!'

'Looks like they used the same method for picking all those pockets too,' called Spud from under the stage.

Lara ducked through the space in the panel. Spud was pointing to a pile of purses and wallets stashed in the corner.

'And look at this!' yapped Star, gazing at the wall of photographs and newspaper clippings. 'Princess Pretty certainly had it in for Summer Rayne!'

'But where's she hidden Cupcake?' Lara wondered. 'Have a good look around. There might be a clue here somewhere.'

Just then, a toilet flushed backstage, followed by footsteps coming closer.

'Uh-oh,' Spud whispered. 'Sounds like Princess Poopy is still here – and she's heading our way!'

12. The Dancing Troll

'Darren? What are you doing here?' Princess Pretty demanded, glaring at the troll standing in the orchestra pit. 'You're supposed to be on the ride with Summer while I deal with Cupcake!'

'Huh?' woofed the troll.

'Oh, you're such an idiot!' grumbled Princess Pretty. 'Well, it's too late now. You'll never make it there in time for the launch. You'll just have to come with me instead.'

Hiding inside the troll costume, Lara felt a mixture of delight and dread. *Just as I'd hoped! Princess Pretty thinks we're Darren, and now she's going to lead us to Cupcake. But how do I make this thing move?* She was standing upright, with her hind legs pushed into the troll boots. Star was perched on her shoulders and Spud on Star's.

'Come on, Darren!' yelled Princess Pretty.

Lara peered out through the mesh square in the troll's chest. Princess Pretty was waiting impatiently by the side door of the theatre. She was wearing the backpack full of money.

'Hold on, pups,' Lara whispered. 'Time to get this troll on the move! You do the arms and I'll do the legs.'

The troll staggered forward for a couple of steps with its huge head swaying from side to side before it got into its stride and waddled out of the theatre after Princess Pretty. Lara forgot to duck and the troll yelped as its huge head hit the door frame.

'What's the matter with you?' hissed Princess Pretty as the troll staggered like it had been hit with a mallet. 'Everyone's looking at us!'

Inside the costume, Lara made a big effort to walk in a straight line, but the doggie trio meant she kept lurching left and then right.

'Look, Mummy! It's a dancing troll!' laughed one little boy as Lara did a side-shuffle back towards Princess Pretty. Spud made the troll wave at the boy. He waved back. A few steps later, Lara lurched to the left again and crashed into a candyfloss stall.

'Whoa!' cried Spud and Star as the heavy troll head pitched forward into the whirling candyfloss machine. They leant back on Lara's shoulders and the troll head rose up from the machine again with a big pink ball of candyfloss stuck on the end of its nose.

Yum, candyfloss!' yapped Spud. 'My favourite!'

Lara staggered on, gasping for breath. Spud was enjoying himself. The troll's arms swung wildly, scooping three ice creams from a nearby stall. *Thanking you.* Two were slapped against its forehead. *Missed*, thought Spud. The third went in its big green mouth. 'Result!' drooled Spud. 'My favourite!' The puppy was getting over-confident. He waved at another child, his huge troll hand wiping out a row of prizes on the hook-a-duck stall. *Whoops! Sorry!*

'Right!' snapped Princess Pretty. 'That's it! We're going the back way.' She sidestepped into an alleyway, forcing Lara to make a wobbly turn and shuffle after her. The crowds streamed on down the main street, heading for the big event of the day: the launch of Storm Spell. Only one person stopped by the alleyway to stare after Princess Pretty and the dancing troll. Darren hesitated, frowning, between the alleyway and the gleaming Storm Spell launch pad at the end of the main street. Then he made his decision; he ducked into the alleyway and followed them into the forest.

108

13. A Race Against Time

Lara staggered into the forest clearing behind
Princess Pretty and collapsed on to the ground
with a groan. Spud and Star climbed down
from her shoulders, and squeezed into the
troll's trousers beside her, letting the troll's
head slump sideways.

'Well done, Ma!' whispered Star. 'You made
it!'

'Shhh!' warned Lara as she heard Princess
Pretty's footsteps coming towards them.

'Poor Darren. Are you tired?' said Princess
Pretty's voice sweetly. 'Why don't you take
off that heavy old troll head?'

'Yeah! Let's do that!' whispered Spud. 'I'd
like to see the look on Princess Potty's face
when we jump out at her!'

'Not yet,' whispered Lara suspiciously.

First I want to see why she's being so nice all of a sudden.' Cautiously, she lifted her head and peered out through the mesh square. Princess Pretty was standing over them gripping a fallen tree branch with both hands. *Hmm. I thought so. She's planning to whack Darren with that branch as soon as he sticks his head out!*

Suddenly a noise behind Princess Pretty made her turn round. She gasped in astonishment as Darren walked into the clearing. 'You! But how . . .?'

'What's going on?' growled Darren, glaring at Princess Pretty. 'Have you been seeing another troll behind my back?'

'No! I thought it was you in there! But – if you're standing here – who's in the troll costume?'

'Let's find out, shall we?' snapped Darren, marching up to the troll. He grabbed the head and yanked it from the body. His expression turned from fury to bewilderment as he stared down at the three dogs sitting side by side in the troll's trousers.

Hi, wagged Star.

Nice to meet you, wagged Spud. *Have you got any sandwiches?*

'Them again!' shrieked Princess Pretty. 'Get them, Darren!'

Darren lunged for Lara, but she was too quick for him. She leapt out of the troll's trousers and shot between his legs. Darren made a grab for Spud and Star and managed to hook a finger through Spud's collar but, quick as a flash, Lara turned and sank her teeth into his bum.

'Ooww!' yelled Darren, dropping Spud and clutching at his backside.

'Look out, Ma!' yelled Star.

Out of the corner of her eye, Lara saw Princess Pretty's branch swinging towards her. She let go of Darren's bum, ducked under the branch and then ran to join Spud and Star. She heard Darren yell as the branch whacked him across the backside.

'You can't be ordinary dogs,' said Princess Pretty, looking at them with suspicion in her eyes.

'No, we're not! We're *extra*ordinary *Spy Dogs!*' yapped Lara, Spud and Star, facing Darren and Princess Pretty across the clearing.

There was a sudden groaning noise and everyone looked round at the brand-new fairground ride. The snap of breaking metal sounded above the trees like a gunshot. One of the huge legs supporting the rollercoaster track was buckling and the rollercoaster seemed to be sinking to its knees.

'W-w-what's happening?' stammered Darren.

'What do you think, stupid?' shrieked Princess Pretty. 'The ride is collapsing.

Because YOU painted that metal leg with acid. So YOU will be responsible when the carriage smashes to the ground.'

'You told me it was paint!' gasped Darren.

'And you believed me! You're even more stupid than I thought!' Princess Pretty looked around at the horrified faces of Darren and the dogs. 'Oh, and sweet little Cupcake is up there,' she cackled, pointing to the highest part of the rollercoaster.

All eyes gazed upwards and, sure enough, they could see a small cage dangling by a rope.

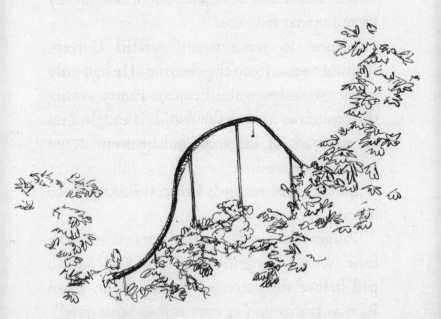

The rollercoaster's wheels cut the rope and little doggie dies. You have to admit, Troll Face, that it's the perfect plan.'

Darren gulped, and his mouth gaped open. He didn't have the fastest mind in the world, but even he could work out that this was not good.

'But – the ride is about to start!' he gasped.

'I know! Bye-bye, Summer Rayne. And toodle-pip, little Cupcake.' Princess Pretty laughed crazily.

Lara sprang to her feet as the Storm Spell rails groaned and buckled. The Cook family were on that ride too!

'I have to warn them!' yelled Darren, turning to run from the clearing. He had only taken two steps when Princess Pretty swung the branch as hard as she could. It caught him on the back of his head and he went down without a sound.

Spud stalked towards Princess Pretty, teeth bared.

'Forget her, Spud!' woofed Lara. 'There's no time. We have to get to the Storm Spell launch pad before the carriages set off! Run, pups! Run as fast as you've ever run in your lives!'

14. Crash!

Ben was grinning so hard, his face was beginning to ache. He could not quite believe that he, Benjamin Cook, was sitting next to superstar Summer Rayne, in the front carriage of a rollercoaster *he* had named; this had to be one of the most thrilling moments of his life! *My friends'll be so envious*, he thought, looking up at the huge sign rising above the launch pad. There it was, in letters three metres high, painted in steel blue and gun-metal grey, with a yellow thunderbolt cutting through the middle.

'You must be very proud and happy, Ben,' said Summer, giving him a warm smile.

'Yeah, I am,' Ben admitted. 'But I feel a bit guilty about it, when you're having such a bad time.'

'Don't be,' said Summer. 'At the end of this ride, I'll get my Cupcake back! Then we'll both be happy.'

There were four carriages on the Storm Spell rollercoaster, each with twelve seats arranged in three rows of four. When the ride was full, it would carry forty-eight people but, for the launch ride, only the first seven seats were taken. Ben was in the very front row, along with Summer Rayne, Ollie and Sophie, and Mr and Mrs Cook were in the second row with Mr Cartwright. Ben glanced back at Mr Cook, who was looking a bit green even before the ride started. 'Sure you don't want to get off, Dad?' he asked.

116

'And miss the launch of the rollercoaster my son named? No chance!' said Mr Cook bravely.

Ben looked across at the Storm Spell viewing platform, which was packed with spectators. He scanned the crowd, looking for a furry black and white face with one sticky-up ear, but Lara wasn't there. Ben knew that Lara, Spud and Star were busy trying to find Cupcake, but he still felt a twinge of disappointment that his friend was not there to watch the launch.

Behind him, Mr Cartwright was speaking into his walkie-talkie. 'Thank you. Over and out,' he finished and clipped the walkie-talkie to his belt. 'Summer? We're ready to launch.'

Summer stood up and turned to face the viewing platform. 'I declare Storm Spell, the biggest rollercoaster in the world, open!' she cried in a loud, clear voice. She cut a pink ribbon and the crowd cheered. The ride attendant lowered the rigid harnesses over the riders' heads and checked that they were locked in place. The TV news cameras were rolling. A helicopter hovered, capturing the new ride from every angle.

'Five!' called Mr Cartwright as the attendant hurried back to the control cubicle.

'FOUR!' yelled the crowd enthusiastically.

Ben looked for Lara one last time.

'THREE!'

He caught a glimpse of a black and white dog racing along the path below. It was Lara, with Spud and Star hot on her heels. She had come to see him off, after all!

'TWO!'

Lara bounded up on to the launch pad and Ben stopped grinning. Something was wrong; he could tell by the frantic look on her face.

'ONE!'

Lara, Spud and Star were barking madly. Spud was shaking his head. Star was holding up her paws in a 'stop' gesture. Lara drew a paw across her throat.

'They want us to stop the launch!' cried Ben, but his words were lost in the roar of the crowd.

'LIFT OFF!'

The Storm Spell rollercoaster lurched forward and set off along the rails, picking up speed. 'No! Stop!' barked Lara as Ben's white face sped past her. She lunged for the control cubicle, yanked the door open and reached for the lever that would stop the ride.

'Help! Mad dog!' cried the terrified attendant, kicking Lara out and then slamming the door in her face.

There was only one thing left to do. Lara raced back to the launch pad. 'Ready, pups?' she barked as the last carriage sped past.

'Ready, Ma!' yapped Spud and Star.

Jump!'

The pups leapt high into the air and landed in a tangled heap in the very last row of seats.

'Brilliant,' howled Lara above the noise of the ride. 'Now, time to use those free-running skills.'

Cupcake was yapping, but nobody was listening. This, she considered, was most unusual. She was used to getting everything she yapped for. Her cage dangled in the wind, the rope trailing across the roller-coaster track. She peered out of the bars at the view below. She could see a big crowd and a small metal carriage just setting off. She squinted and could just make out Summer, sitting in the front seat. *Oh, goody*, thought the little dog. *They're sending a rescue team. About time too!*

The ride climbed steadily, click-clicking its way to the highest point.

Lara was sprinting along the ground under the tracks. She knew there were only seconds to go before the wheels would cut through the rope and Cupcake would plunge to her death.

In the front carriage, Ben tried to twist round in his seat, but the rigid harness was holding him in place. 'Mr Cartwright!' he screamed.

What's the matter, Ben?' the old man called.

'Something's wrong! You have to stop the ride!'

The carriage approached the crest of the slope. The view was magnificent. Nobody could see Cupcake dangling from a rope.

'But it's completely safe, Ben! We've tested everything over and over again!'

'Please, Mr Cartwright!' Ben begged as they reached the top of the loop. 'Use your walkie-talkie and get them to stop the ride!'

'I can't do that, Ben,' Mr Cartwright said firmly. 'Not without a good reason.'

Ben flung his head back in frustration. At the top of the loop, a huge mirror had been rigged up over the rails so that the riders could see their own terrified faces just before they plunged down the other side. Ben could see all the empty carriages behind him. Except they weren't empty! Spud and Star were leaping from seat to seat, working their way up the carriages towards the front.

'Is that a good enough reason?' yelled Ben, pointing up at the mirror.

Mr Cartwright looked up, turned deathly

pale and reached for his walkie-talkie. 'Stop the ride!' he yelled as Spud and Star soared towards him. 'There are dogs aboard! Stop the ride!'

The carriage seemed to stop momentarily before its wheels severed the rope and the ride tipped over on to the steep downward slope.

Whoosh! Spud and Star slammed the harnesses down over themselves, hooked their legs through and grabbed the crossbars with their teeth. A split second later, the world went into a spin.

What followed were the longest ten seconds of the pups' lives. Spud's liking for ice cream and sausages meant his harness fitted quite well. He managed a doggie grin as they went upside down. *Whoo-hoo!* Star hung on, but could feel her legs slipping through the bars. First one back leg, then the other, flew up into the air and she was left hanging on by her front paws and her teeth. When the spinning finally stopped, she collapsed into the seat next to Spud, feeling as though all her bones had turned to water. 'That was no fun at all,' she groaned, slamming her harness into place.

The carriages started to climb again. Was Star imagining it, or did they seem to be slowing down?

'It's all right, pups!' Ben cried from the front row. 'Mr Cartwright has told them to stop the ride!'

Thank goodness, thought Star, slumping back in her seat. *We did it!*

'Sis?' quavered Spud, pointing at the track.

Star looked and felt her heart jump up into her throat. They were over the forest now and, only a short distance ahead, the tracks were a buckled, twisted mess of metal.

The carriages were slowing, the brakes screeching. But the gap was coming at them awfully fast.

15. The Leap of Faith

Princess Pretty hooked her hands under Darren's arms and dragged his unconscious body across the clearing until he was lying directly under the twisted section of the Storm Spell tracks.

'You just *crash* out there,' she said, sniggering at her own joke as she patted his face. 'It'll all be over soon!'

Everything was going well. The dogs had bolted so Princess Pretty settled the backpack full of money more comfortably on her shoulders and set off for a nearby hill. She reached a decent viewpoint and sat down just as the rumble of the speeding Storm Spell ride began to echo across the treetops. Her eyes glittered as she watched the carriage reach its highest point and the cage fell. 'Yes!' She cocked her

hand to her ear and thought she heard a satis-
fying yowl as Cupcake fell to her death. Then
she watched as the blue and grey carriages
whirled and looped towards the forest, and
she rubbed her hands together as the damaged
support leg bent even further to the ground,
splitting the track in two.

'Perfect!' she crowed, looking from the
broken track to the carriages, but then her
forehead creased into a frown. The ride was
slowing down! 'Don't you dare stop!' she
yelled, jumping to her feet, but the carriages
kept on slowing. There were sparks and a
terrible screeching sound as the brakes were
applied. Princess Pretty watched in horror as
the train crept towards the break in the track.
It very nearly stopped in time, but then the
front of the first carriage tipped over the
broken edge of the rail. Princess Pretty held
her breath, willing it to fall, but the carriage
came to a halt, half on and half off the rail.
It hung there, delicately balanced, swaying
gently, high above the ground.

Spud opened first one eye, then the other.
Still alive! he thought. *I can't quite believe it!*

He could hear the groan and creak of metal, but otherwise, it was strangely quiet. He noticed it was windy this high up. He looked at the seat next to him. Star was curled into a ball, eyes tightly shut, waiting for the impact.

'Has anyone seen my stomach?' said Spud faintly. 'I think I left it behind back there.'

Star opened her eyes. 'Are we safe now?'

'Erm. Not exactly,' said her brother, looking at the drop they were hanging over.

Other noises began to fill the silence. Mr Cartwright's walkie-talkie started to squawk, metal creaked and the TV news helicopter hovered. Ollie started to cry.

'Shhh. It's all right,' soothed Mrs Cook automatically.

'I don't understand,' said Mr Cartwright in a dazed voice. 'We checked everything. How did this happen?'

'Never mind that,' said Mr Cook. 'We're still alive, thanks to Lara, Spud and Star, but now we need to get to the back of this carriage before it tips over the edge! Everyone, on the count of three, unlock your harnesses. No sudden movements! One, two, three!'

With a click, the harnesses unlocked and lifted above their heads. The carriage rocked and the rails groaned, but they stayed in place.

'Good,' said Mr Cook. 'Now, we're going to move to the back one by one, starting with you, Ollie. Are you ready?'

'Yes, Dad,' quavered Ollie.

'Good boy. Off you go.'

Slowly, Ollie slipped from his seat and

edged his way to the back, where he buried his face in Star's fur. Sophie went next, then Ben, then Summer. The rails groaned and the carriage rocked alarmingly. Finally, as Mr and Mrs Cook and Mr Cartwright edged towards the back, the balance shifted and the carriage settled back more firmly on to the rails.

They moved more quickly after that. With Spud and Star leading the way, they clambered from carriage to carriage until finally, everyone was at the back.

'What now?' asked Summer.

'We wait for rescue,' said Mr Cartwright. 'Look, the news helicopter is lowering a rope ladder.'

Just then, the damaged supporting leg moved again, leaning further towards the trees and the whole ride lurched to one side.

'No time to wait!' cried Ben. 'We have to get off the carriage.'

One by one the passengers climbed out of the carriage and assembled on the track. Mr Cook was last out. As he climbed out, he accidentally kicked the carriage and that was enough to send it crashing to the forest floor.

The small group huddled together as the earth shook.

'Not quite as planned,' sobbed Summer Rayne. 'But at least we're alive.'

16. The Ride of Your Life

Lara wasn't sure if she'd get there in time. Her lungs were bursting as she dashed through the undergrowth. She heard a groan nearby. *Good, Darren's awake. I need all the help I can get!*

Darren sprang to his feet as Lara galloped into the clearing. She skidded to a halt and

pointed skywards. They both looked up and saw the carriage approaching the highest point of the ride. *Just a few seconds before Cupcake falls*, Lara thought. She heard the click-clicking stop. *Yikes, they're at the top!*

'Oh no!' yelled Darren, gazing up at the cage. 'Cupcake!'

Lara didn't have time to think. She grabbed the troll's trousers by one of the braces and dragged them over to Darren.

'Good thinking, doggie!' cried Darren, grabbing the other brace. Lara stood on her hind legs and, together, they opened the trousers as far as they would go. *Paws crossed*, Lara thought. *It's not perfect, but it's the best I can do!*

Lara gulped as the small cage dropped. It was very high up. *This is going to be a close call*, she thought as she and Darren ran left and right, trying to judge exactly where Cupcake would fall. *Right*, Lara panted. *No left. And left a bit more!* At the halfway point Lara could hear the terrified yowl of Cupcake. *Left a bit more.* Lara and Darren opened the troll's trousers as wide as they would go. *Thud!* Lara was flattened as Cupcake's cage landed. *A direct hit*, she whistled, righting herself. *I hardly dare look!*

'Did we do it?' asked Darren. 'Did we save Cupcake?'

Lara peered into the trousers.

'What on earth are you gawping at, mongrel?' yapped Cupcake. 'For goodness' sake get me out of this cage! And these ridiculous troll's trousers.'

Lara smiled. *No need to thank me, little mutt. All in a day's work for a Spy Dog!*

Princess Pretty watched with delight as the carriage crashed down from the rails. The ground shook, a tree toppled and pieces of metal whizzed over her head. A huge cloud of dust mushroomed into the air, which was filled with the sound of screaming steel.

She was disappointed to see the small crowd of passengers huddled high up on the track. 'I guess you can't have everything,' she cursed. 'But at least I have the cash. Hollywood, here I come!'

Lara looked up at the whirring helicopter. A ladder was dangling and she could see Sophie clinging on. Ben gave her a thumbs up. *Phew!* she thought as Darren opened the cage and gently lifted Cupcake out. *Looks like everyone's being rescued. Now for Princess Potty!*

Lara stood up and looked around. She spotted a figure in a pink dress standing on top of a small hill. *Got you. No getting away this time – I have a troll on my side!* She looked at Darren and pointed to the hill.

'I see her,' said Darren, tucking Cupcake firmly under his arm. 'Let's go!'

'Put me down!' wailed Cupcake as Darren and Lara raced towards the hill.

'Sorry, Cupcake,' woofed Lara as Princess Pretty turned and ran. 'We have a baddie to catch!'

'She's heading for the theme park,' panted Darren.

They burst out of the forest just as Princess Pretty reached the edge of the park. The baddie ran full pelt into the crowd, knocking over a small child and punching a woman in the face as she went. 'Out of my way!' she screamed.

Princess Pratface doesn't care who she hurts, does she? thought Lara. *Left! She's gone left!* she noted as she spotted the pink dress bobbing through the crowds.

They sprinted after her and burst out on to the pedestrian street next to the log flume. Lara skidded to a halt, looking for a pink dress. *There she goes! And she's got the rucksack with her.*

Princess Pretty was forcing her way up the steps to the log flume, pushing people out of her way. She reached the wooden quayside where the logs were moored.

'Ticket?' asked the attendant, holding out his hand.

Princess Pretty whacked him with the money bag and he fell into the water. She leapt on to a waiting log.

Darren sprinted away down the hill, with Cupcake still howling under his arm.

He's heading for the end of the flume ride, thought Lara. *Good! Pincer movement! I'll stick with Princess – if I can make it in time!* She noticed a high fence with 'Wild West Log Ride' nailed to it. *Short cut!* She clawed her way to the top of the fence, cat-style, and launched herself. 'Geronimo!' barked Lara as she disappeared over the top of the fence. She thumped into an empty log. *Perfect landing! Now for the chase.* The current picked them up and they were swirled into a downhill torrent of water. Lara swished her paws through the water, paddling hard.

Princess Pretty looked round. Her face twisted into a snarl of fury when she spotted Lara in the log behind.

They swirled round a few corners and through a dark tunnel, all the time Lara gaining on Princess Pretty and the ransom money. The ride was almost at an end when Lara decided to go for it. *It's now or never!* She crouched at the front of the log and sprang, just as the flume plunged downwards in its final splash. A camera flashed, there was a mini tidal wave and the ride ended with Lara sitting on top of the evil baddie, money bag safely in her jaws. Darren cheered. Lara bowed.

All the fight had gone out of Princess Pretty, but Lara sat on her until the security guards arrived, just in case. As Darren was explaining the situation, a Land Rover pulled up and Summer Rayne jumped out, followed by the Cooks and Mr Cartwright.

'Cupcake!' cried Summer, running straight past the backpack of money to scoop the little dog up in her arms. The crowd began to take photographs.

'No pictures!' squeaked Cupcake, for the first time in her life. Summer opened her shoulder bag and the little dog dived gratefully inside.

'I'm so sorry, Mr Cartwright,' cried Darren.

'I've been a fool! I had no idea she was planning this!' He burst into tears.

Lara felt sorry for Darren. He was just a big stupid lump who had fallen in love with the wrong woman.

'I believe you, son,' said Mr Cartwright. 'She had us all fooled.'

Huh! Speak for yourself, thought Lara.

'It wasn't me — it was him!' screamed Princess Pretty, pointing at Darren. 'He did it all! And no one can prove otherwise!'

In response, Lara stuck her nose into Summer's bag and detached the bottom part of the camera locket on Cupcake's collar with her teeth. She trotted over to Mr Cartwright and dropped the plug-in memory stick into his hand.

Mr Cartwright hurried over to the control cubicle of the flume ride and plugged in the memory stick. A few seconds later, the big screens all over Enchanted Towers Theme Park were showing images of Princess Pretty's snarling face as she roped Cupcake's cage to the rollercoaster.

'Well, she got what she wanted,' woofed Lara. 'She's the star of the big screen!'

Princess Pretty let out an off-key wail and Darren screwed up his face at the noise. 'I've been wanting to tell you this for ages,' he said. 'You can't sing, Princess. You can't sing for toffee!'

'Oh, I recognize you now!' said Summer Rayne, staring at Princess Pretty's wide open mouth. 'You're the chorus girl from my first musical!'

'Yes!' hissed Princess Pretty. 'And you stopped the director from giving me the star role!'

Summer Rayne looked bewildered. 'Actually, I persuaded him to give you a place in the chorus.'

'Rubbish! He told me he'd never heard anything like my singing!'

'He meant it too,' said Summer. 'He said that when you sang, you honked like a goose!'

Princess Pretty wailed even more loudly as she was led away to the police van, forcing everyone to stuff their fingers in their ears.

'Honks like a goose? I think that's an insult to our feathered friends,' woofed Lara.

The flume ride manager presented Lara with her official ride photo, taken at the top of the final drop. It had captured her sailing through the air towards Princess Pretty. 'One for your scrapbook,' he suggested.

Lara puffed out her chest. *A Spy Dog always gets her baddie!*

The pups were curled up together, gently snoring. Star was twitching, dreaming of her rollercoaster brush with death. Spud wore a satisfied smile, his belly heaving up and down, swollen with his chicken curry reward.

'Check this out, Lara,' said Ben, pointing at the news. 'It's us!' And sure enough, there were the Cooks, waving to the TV helicopter. 'Our job is to tell the news,' said the reporter. 'It's not often we get to *make* the news,' he grinned. 'And it's not every day that we get to rescue a pop star from a rollercoaster catastrophe. I guess it was a case of right place, right time.'

Lara whistled softly as she watched the footage of the news helicopter winching the survivors aboard. 'These were today's dramatic scenes as pop star Summer Rayne was rescued from the mangled wreckage of the world's fastest fairground ride.' Summer's face lit up the TV as she beamed at her rescuers. 'How's that for a rock and roller-coaster!' grimaced the news reader, wishing he didn't have to read out other people's scripts.

Cool ending, thought Lara.

Ben looked across at his pet dog and grinned. 'You, Mrs Retired Spy Dog, caught her red-handed. Plus the video evidence from Cupcake's collar means the police have a watertight case!'

Lara stretched with pride, her bullet-holed ear standing proud.

'And Cupcake?' asked Ollie. 'The cute little hound. Is she OK?'

Lara cast a disapproving look at Ollie. *Little maybe*, she thought. *But cute? Never. And the worst doggie attitude ever!*

'She's been temporarily rehoused,' explained Sophie. 'On a farm in Wales. Summer's going on tour and she thinks Cupcake needs to recuperate after her fall.'

Lara grinned a huge doggie grin on the inside that showed as a lolloping tongue on the outside. Her eyes sparkled as she considered Cupcake's new surroundings. *Imagine the mud! And the sheep dogs! Maybe she'll learn some manners?*

Lara lay down and put her head between her paws. *Rescuing people from crashed roller-coasters and catching baddies on log flumes is exhausting work!* Her eyes were already half closed. She cast one more look at Ben, Sophie and Ollie. *Adventure is great*, she thought. *But families are better!*

**Turn over the page to get your paws on
a sneaky peek at the first chapter of**

SPY
PUPS
TRAINING SCHOOL

1. The Mask with Two Faces

'Follow me, folks!' the museum guide called. 'You're about to see one of the most important pieces of art in the whole world – and we're proud to have it on display in our very own Metropolitan Museum of Art, right here in New York!'

A crowd of tourists and a teacher with a party of schoolchildren followed the guide through a narrow tunnel into a round, windowless room. A circle in the middle of the room was roped off, leaving a strip of open floor around the edge. As the crowd shuffled in and lined up behind the rope barrier, two men in dark suits slipped into the room and stood behind the crowd, one on either side of the tunnel.

If anyone had looked at the pair, they would

have had a shock. The two men were identical in every detail, except that one had a mole on his right cheek and the other had exactly the same mole on his left cheek. Nobody did look, though; they were all too busy peering at the shadowy object roped off in the middle of the room.

'Here we go,' said the guide. 'Feast your eyes on the Janus mask!' He flicked a switch and a powerful spotlight snapped on.

The crowd gasped. The mask in the centre of the room was made of pure beaten gold; it gleamed softly as it turned on its pedestal. It

had two identical faces, one at the front and one at the back.

'Can I try it on?' asked a small girl.

'Sorry, sweetie,' said the guide. 'This isn't a fancy dress mask. It's priceless! It dates back to early Roman times and it's the only one of its kind.'

A boy raised his hand. 'Why does it have two faces?'

'Good question, son,' said the guide. 'Janus was a Roman god who could see both forward into the future and backward into the past, so the mask-maker gave him two faces. You could say Janus had eyes in the back of his head, just like your teacher here!'

The schoolchildren giggled.

'Yes, I do,' agreed the teacher. 'That's how I know some of you are eating candy right now, even though I told you no food in the museum!'

The children stopped giggling and there was a rustling as sweets were reluctantly pushed back into pockets. The adults in the crowd chuckled and then everyone turned back to studying the golden mask.

Everyone except the two dark-suited men. They were busy checking out the museum security instead. Their cold blue eyes took in the lasers, the security cameras and the pressure pad under the mask. Finally, they both focused on a thin steel ring set into the floor around the pedestal. They frowned. The steel ring was something new. What was it for? What did it do? Their eyes met and they both gave the slightest of shrugs.

Just then a boy in front of the men eased a bag of jelly babies back out of his pocket. The pair shared a smile and then bent down, one on each side of the boy.

'Teacher said no candy, kid!' hissed one of the men.

The boy jumped and, at the same time, the other man nudged his arm. A jelly baby flew from the bag, sailed over the rope barrier and bounced on to the floor beside the steel ring. The two men watched with interest to see what would happen next.

The jelly baby was instantly sliced in half as a cylinder shot up out of the steel ring. The cylinder zoomed upwards with a metallic hiss and locked into a groove in the roof, sealing the Janus mask behind a pillar of steel.

In the moment of stunned silence that

followed, one of the dark-suited men plucked the remaining jelly babies from the boy's hand. The boy began to cry.

'Simon!' roared the teacher. 'Was that your jelly baby?'

'It wasn't my fault! It was those nasty men!'

Simon turned and pointed behind him, but there was nobody there. The men had slipped away.

'Jelly baby, Brad?'

'Thanks, Chad. Don't mind if I do.'

Brad and Chad Onkers strolled away from the museum into Central Park, chewing on Simon's jelly babies. They found a quiet bench and sat down side by side.

'We must,' began Brad.

'Have that mask,' finished Chad.

'It's us!' began Brad.

'In gold!' finished Chad.

The Onkers twins turned on the bench so that they were back to back, and posed as the Janus mask. It was a spooky sight. Their spiky blond hair was exactly the same length and thickness, their noses had identical bumps across the bridge, and their chins both had a cleft down the middle which made them look like tiny bums. The only way to tell them apart was their moles.

'So. It's agreed. We steal,' began Chad.

'The Janus mask,' finished Brad.

'In time for,' began Chad.

'Our birthday next week,' finished Brad.

'Better than any cake!' they said together.

'But how,' asked Brad.

'Do we do it?' finished Chad.

'It'll be our toughest job yet,' said Brad.

'Let's think on it,' said Chad.

They sat on the bench until they had finished Simon's jelly babies, then they both shook their heads and stood up.

'Nothing yet,' said Chad.

'Me neither,' admitted Brad. 'We'll figure it out. We always do. Meanwhile, I gotta get to work.' He pulled an FBI badge from his pocket and hung it round his neck. The badge had his photograph on one side, and the words SPECIAL AGENT B. ONKERS on the other.

'I gotta get to work too,' said Chad, pulling a set of skeleton keys from his pocket and running them through his fingers.

'What's the heist this time?' asked Brad.

'Those two Picasso paintings in the mansion you were protecting a few months back.'

Brad's blue eyes gleamed greedily. 'They'll look lovely hanging on our wall. You got the codes for the burglar alarm?'

Chad nodded and tapped the side of his head. 'It's all in here. The layout of the mansion — everything. That night I spent there posing as you was very useful. You know, Brad, every art thief should have a twin working in the FBI!'

'And every FBI agent should have a twin working as an art thief!

'Two heads are better than one,' said Chad.

'Or two faces,' said Brad.

The Onkers twins leant their identical faces together and gave an identical evil laugh.